**"DO YOU [...]
TO ME?"**

"Tell me," she whispered recklessly. She tilted her head to explore the throbbing pulse in his throat with her lips.

"You're setting me on fire."

The fire of passion, the throb of desire . . . yes, she felt that too!

With a soft growl deep in his throat, he suddenly swept her up in his arms, and then nothing else mattered as their passion was unleashed, flame recklessly meeting flame to rage higher and higher in a wildfire of desire. . . .

Lisa McConnell was born in the Pacific Northwest and has lived there most of her life. She presently resides only a few miles from the Rogue River, spectacular setting of *River of Love*. In addition to enjoying the river, Ms. McConnell also enjoys travel, horseback riding, motorcycling with her husband, plus both reading and writing romantic love stories.

Dear Reader:

Signet has always been known for its consistently fine individual romances, and now we are proud to introduce a provocative new line of contemporary romances, RAPTURE ROMANCE. While maintaining our high editorial standards, RAPTURE ROMANCE will explore all the possibilities that exist when today's men and women fall in love. Mutual respect, gentle affection, raging passion, tormenting jealousy, overwhelming desire, and finally, pure rapture—the moods of romance will be vividly presented in the kind of sensual yet always tasteful detail that makes a fantasy real. We are very enthusiastic about RAPTURE ROMANCE, and we hope that you will enjoy reading these novels as much as we enjoy finding and publishing them for you!

In fact, please let us know what you do think—we love to hear from our readers, and what you tell us about your likes and dislikes is taken seriously. We have enclosed a questionnaire with some of our own queries at the back of this book. Please take a few minutes to fill it out, or if you prefer, write us directly at the address below.

And don't forget that your favorite RAPTURE ROMANCE authors need your encouragement; although we can't give out addresses, we will be happy to forward any mail.

We look forward to hearing from you!

> Robin Grunder
> RAPTURE ROMANCE
> New American Library
> 1633 Broadway
> New York, NY 10019

RIVER
OF
LOVE

by

Lisa McConnell

RAPTURE ROMANCE

NEW AMERICAN LIBRARY

TIMES MIRROR

PUBLISHER'S NOTE

This novel is a work of fiction. Names, characters, places, and
incidents are either the product of the author's imagination or
are used fictitiously, and any resemblance to actual persons,
living or dead, events, or locales is entirely coincidental.

SIGNET, SIGNET CLASSICS, MENTOR, PLUME, MERIDIAN AND NAL
BOOKS are published by The New American Library, Inc.,
1633 Broadway, New York, New York 10019

First Printing, January, 1983

1 2 3 4 5 6 7 8 9

PRINTED IN THE UNITED STATES OF AMERICA

Chapter One

Rain. Water streamed down the windshield, the swishing wiper blades barely able to keep a space clear so Lark could see the freeway ahead of her. Water sheeted the asphalt, the pounding drops turning the roadway into a silvery river. A van passed Lark's small car, and she smiled ruefully when she saw the bumper sticker. It read "Oregonians Don't Tan—They Rust." That certainly seemed a possibility, considering the wet, stormy Oregon weather she had encountered so far.

Perhaps she had been too hasty, too impulsive, she thought, doubt assailing her again as she peered through the spray of another passing car. Right now she could have been planning her wedding, looking forward to a calm, secure future as a young dentist's wife. Instead, here she was on a rainswept freeway somewhere in southwestern Oregon, with only a few dollars in her pocket, heading for an uncertain future rooming with a schoolmate she hadn't seen in several years, in a city she had never even visited.

But she had to do it this way, she thought with an almost panicky sense of desperation. She had to get away before she took the path of least resistance and married Stanley on the basis of gratitude and logic. She was so weary of coping with the legacy of troubles, financial, legal, and moral, that her father had left her. It would have been so *sensible* to marry Stanley.

She was so lost in thought that the exit sign loomed ahead of her with startling suddenness. Lark braked and cut the wheel sharply to make the exit turn, earning an angry honk from the driver behind her.

Once off the freeway, she pulled over to the side of the road, across from a gas station and grocery store, and studied the rather cryptic map Jeanne Denton had drawn for her last summer. The scrawled lines showed a place called Indian Mary Park, then a turnoff and several forks in the road before winding up at a spot marked with an X.

For a moment Lark hesitated. She hadn't heard from Mike and Jeanne since last summer, and they weren't really much more than acquaintances. Perhaps their urging to stop in and visit if she ever got down to southern Oregon was merely one of those meaningless, general invitations people sometimes issue, never dreaming the recipient might really take them up on it. If that was the case, they were certainly going to be surprised, Lark thought wryly, because she intended to spend the night with them. She had little more than enough money to buy gas to get to southern California, and she certainly could not afford high-priced motels along the way. She wished she could telephone ahead, but they had said their secluded cabin had no telephone.

She opened a window and peered around before continuing on her way. The rain still poured down, but the April air had an invigorating freshness. The forested hillsides were incredibly green. She arched her back, trying to relieve the weariness and tension brought on by the day-long drive down from Seattle.

She spread the wrinkled map on the seat beside her and pulled back onto the road. She passed a lumber mill and a few small stores. Somehow she had expected Indian Mary Park to be within a mile or two of the freeway, but the road went on and on. The scenery grew wilder and more rugged. The rocky, wooded slopes rose inches from her window, and here and there she caught glimpses of a frothing, turbulent river rushing headlong through rocky gashes and canyons. She crossed a bridge and finally passed the lovely green park where a few sturdy camp trailers were parked in spite of the miserable weather.

A little farther on she located the turnoff, but by then her lifted spirits were turning to worried concern. Darkness would fall soon, and she must find Mike and Jeanne's cabin before then or she would never locate it on these narrow, twisting mountain roads.

Cautiously she moved on, peering doubtfully up the steep slopes. The rain had let up somewhat, but the clouds had lowered until misty wisps trailed through the treetops above her. Then, off to the side of the road, she spotted the remains of a tumbledown rail fence and a rutted driveway. She checked the map. Yes, this must be the place, because there was the huge pine tree Jeanne had noted.

Relieved, Lark eased the little car onto the dirt road. It did not look well-traveled, but Mike and Jeanne had said they were sick of city life and intended leaving their little cabin as seldom as possible. Driving on, Lark could understand their infatuation with the area. There was something soothing and peaceful about the silent, rain-drenched forest on either side, a sort of aloof, timeless permanence that put mundane problems into proper perspective.

But suddenly she realized with dismay that a very definite problem lay just ahead of her. It was a huge, muddy puddle covering the entire roadway. There was no way to detour around it, and it was impossible to tell how deep the puddle was or how soft the bottom. Lark braked uncertainly, reluctant to attempt to drive across the wet expanse. Finally, after slipping a light jacket over her turtleneck sweater and tying a cotton bandanna over her shoulder-length blond hair, she got out and used a stick to probe warily at the muddy water. She was relieved to find the water only a few inches deep and the bottom hard and solid. She could cross the puddle safely enough. But what else lay ahead? She walked on up the steep road, hoping that once she reached the next curve she would be able to see the cabin. But when she got there, all she saw through the misty drizzle was another curve farther on.

She was standing there trying to decide what to do when the blast of a horn startled her. She turned and hurried back down the road, but the horn blasted again before she reached the curve.

"I'm coming!" she called. Whoever was behind that horn certainly could not number patience among his virtues.

The man, pacing impatiently around her small car, turned to look as she approached. He was tall, ruggedly built, dark-haired, and scowling. His big pickup loomed behind her little car like a giant over a pygmy. His eyes raked over her in a calculated appraisal. Lark stopped short in dismay, suddenly realizing what a vulnerable position she was in here all alone. She did, however, have the road blocked, she realized guiltily, so perhaps he had a right to be impatient and scowling.

She gave him her most winning smile, the one her father always said could melt the ice from the most glacial heart, male or female. "Hi! I'm sorry I'm in your way. I'll move my car. Are you a friend of Mike and Jeanne's? I'm going up to visit them."

Lark's smile had no effect on him, however, and his response was as curt and hostile as his eyes: "Please move your car."

Lark had started to open her car door, but she stopped short, surprised by the unfriendliness in his voice. It was not the usual reaction to her most winning smile.

He was a good six feet tall, and an open-throated plaid shirt emphasized the powerful width of his shoulders. His close-fitting Levi's rode low on lean hips and stretched taut across muscular thighs. His hair was just a shade short of black and his dark eyes watched Lark coldly from beneath heavy brows. The cold hostility of his eyes and his scowl could not conceal his rugged good looks, nor did the harsh, uncompromising line of his mouth hide the sensuousness of his lips, but Lark found his absolute lack of reaction to her friendly smile disconcerting.

She tried again. "I just stopped to see how deep the puddle was before driving through it. It looked as if it might swallow my little car without a trace."

No reaction, not even the hint of a smile. If anything, the unfriendly eyes even narrowed slightly. He just stood there, arms folded, waiting, ignoring the rain falling lightly around him. Finally he raised one dark eyebrow a fraction of an inch, questioning her delay, and Lark hastily reached for the door.

She thought the door was shut tight, but evidently the latch hadn't caught, and the door swung open much more easily than she expected. She stumbled backward, flinging one arm wildly to maintain her balance. She stifled a gasp of pain as her hand struck a wild blackberry bush and thorns ripped deep into her flesh. Then the stab of pain was forgotten as the man's hand shot out to steady her and she felt his harsh grip on her shoulder.

Their eyes caught and held, hers startled and suddenly frightened, his arrogant and oddly mocking. An electric shiver of awareness quivered through Lark as she felt the heat and strength of his grip, an awareness of a hard, compelling virility about him that emphasized her own soft vulnerability. Slowly, as if he had every right to examine her at his leisure, his gaze roamed boldly from her eyes to her mouth and on to the revealing curve of her sweater. Angrily she jerked out of his numbing grasp and slid behind the wheel of her car.

She turned the key and pumped the gas pedal, nervously watching him in the rearview mirror. He had moved back to lean against the fender of the big pickup.

He stood there with arms folded again, expression derisively amused, as if pleased he had angered her. The engine didn't catch, and she tried again, working the pedal vigorously. This time the engine started, but she nervously let the clutch pedal out too fast and the car jerked forward and died. The man in her rearview mirror looked as if he had expected some such incompetence. She tried again, pumping the pedal almost frantically as her hands grew wet and slippery against the steering wheel.

A tap on the glass stopped her, and reluctantly she rolled down the window.

"You've flooded the engine," he advised with an infuriating air of superiority. "There's no point grinding away at it like that. You'll just have to let it sit for a few minutes."

He was leaning over to peer into the window, a strong, capable-looking hand resting on the car door. His face was only inches away from Lark's and she swallowed uneasily. Up close, she saw that his damp hair had a crisp, healthy sheen, and the faint aroma of some masculine shaving lotion clung to his skin. His eyelashes were thick and straight, and the open throat of his shirt revealed a darkly masculine curl of hair. There was a powerful male vitality about him that she found unnerving, but the vibrations of unfriendliness were even more intense.

"Yes, I suppose you're right. I've flooded the engine." She switched the ignition off and sat there with her hands gripping the wheel nervously, flustered and puzzled by his obvious antagonism toward her. After a few moments of awkward silence, she finally asked nervously, "Do you live around here?"

"Native Oregonian," he replied laconically.

That did not exactly answer her question, but she did not press the point. "I think perhaps the car will start now," she stated.

Slowly and carefully she turned the key and started

the car, resisting the nervous impulse to hurry the procedure. The man stepped back, still unsmiling, and a dismaying thought occurred to Lark. If he was driving up this road, he must also be going to see Mike and Jeanne. The prospect of spending any length of time in his company was not one she relished.

"Are you . . . I mean, do you have business up this road?" she asked tentatively.

For the first time, his lips twisted into the suggestion of a humorless smile, and there was a glint of dark amusement in his eyes. An amusement that was somehow more disturbing than reassuring. "You might say I'm . . . ah . . . planning to pay your friends a surprise visit," he said.

"Oh. I see." But Lark didn't really "see" at all. She had the distinct feeling there was some sort of double meaning implied in his words, some private joke perhaps. She put the car in gear. "I'll just move out of your way, then," she said coolly. She turned her attention to the car, deliberately ending the conversation.

The car sloshed safely through the puddle, but there was no place on the far side to pull off and let the pickup pass, and she had to keep going. The big pickup loomed in her rearview mirror like some menacing mechanical monster. Her eyes searched frantically for some place to pull off, but a creek on one side and a rocky slope on the other barred any escape. Finally she found a narrow niche in the slope and managed to squeeze her little car far enough to one side to let the pickup pass.

The man stopped the pickup alongside Lark's car. "Your car running all right now?" he called.

"Yes, it's fine. Everything's fine," Lark replied, brushing a damp palm against her jeans. The last few minutes of driving had been more nerve-racking than the entire day's drive from Seattle.

"Oh? Everything is fine?" He raised a skeptical eyebrow, giving him a darkly satyric look. Unexpectedly he laughed, a humorless, derisive sound. "Perhaps," he said enigmatically.

The pickup lurched forward suddenly, spraying rocks and mud and leaving Lark puzzled and uneasy. She was suddenly aware that her injured hand throbbed and ached. She dug at the imbedded thorns, but they had broken off below skin level and her prying only made the pain worse. She wrapped a handkerchief around the hand to soak up the oozing blood and was just ready to put the car in gear, when she hesitated. If she went ahead now, she would surely again encounter the man at the cabin. Or she might meet him returning on the narrow road, and that possibility was not one she relished either.

She glanced at her watch, then at the darkening mist overhead. She could wait here for a few minutes until he exited. She could still hear the faint sounds of the pickup engine far up the hillside.

Restlessly she slid out of the car. The actual rain had stopped, but the damp mist was so heavy that droplets collected on her hair. Again she puzzled over the man's strange, unfriendly attitude. Perhaps he was some sort of hermit or eccentric recluse? Lark immediately rejected that thought. There was a certain aura of worldly experience about his dark good looks and self-assured appraisal of her that told her he was not adverse to partaking of the pleasures of feminine charms. She had read in his dark, mocking eyes that he found her attractive. Why the hostility?

She dismissed the puzzling question. She didn't care what he thought. She glanced at her watch again, her thoughts turning elsewhere. Stanley would surely have found the note and the ring by now. A ring she should never have accepted in the first place, she thought unhappily as she slid back into the car.

Accepting the ring hadn't been fair to him. But then, she thought with a small flare of resentment, Stanley really hadn't been fair to her either. He had pressed the ring on her at a time when she felt indebted to him, felt she owed him more than just an inadequate word of thanks. Damn her father anyway, for putting her in that position!

As quickly as that thought flashed through her mind, she guiltily regretted it. Her father was dead now. There was no use condemning him for what he was.

And what he was, Lark sighed to herself, was a cheerful, charming con man. When Lark's mother was alive, she had somehow managed to steer that charm into constructive channels, to encourage the practical projects and discourage the wildly inappropriate ones. But Mrs. McIntyre had died when Lark was only twelve years old. After that had come her father's two disastrous marriages and divorces and a whole series of equally disastrous business ventures, everything from selling gold-mining stocks of dubious authenticity and value to involvement in some sort of shady insurance scheme. They had moved often, from Arizona's desert country to Florida's beaches and New York's big-city sophistication.

Lark thought everything had changed when her father settled in Seattle, Washington, and got into a land-subdivision and housing-development project a couple of years ago. It was an ambitious project involving the reclamation of some hundred acres of swampy lowland for housing. She and her father lived in a model home on the project grounds, and Lark gave prospective customers tours of the house and drove them around the land in a sleek Cadillac. Lark had never really understood how the whole project was financed, but occasionally her father had important business meetings with prosperous-looking people, and there always seemed to be plenty of money.

Lark met Stanley when he was considering buying a house. He kept coming back to look, though he never bought, and he finally admitted he was coming to see her instead of the property. Lark liked Stanley, and they started dating occasionally, though she felt more sisterly than romantic toward him.

Then things started to go wrong for her father. First

came the insistent phone calls, which he wouldn't discuss with Lark but which obviously upset him. Then the complaints started coming in: inferior construction materials, leaking roofs, faulty electrical wiring, cracking foundations. Investigators began sniffing around; a lawsuit was filed against Lark's father. Still he kept smiling, telling her not to worry her pretty head about such things.

And then everything fell apart. First the stunning, horrifying auto accident. Lark had barely begun to assimilate the reality of her father's death when everything else deluged upon her. She learned the finances surrounding the housing development were a tangled web and she was caught in the middle. Her father had somehow pledged assets on which he already owed money to secure other debts. Property titles were clouded. People called day and night with complaints.

Lark didn't know what to do or where to turn, and that was when Stanley stepped in. He helped her find a competent, trustworthy lawyer. He offered a solid shoulder to cry on, a sympathetic ear. He wanted her to marry him immediately when the model home in which she lived was lost in the foreclosure, but he helped her find a tiny apartment when she said she just couldn't think about marriage yet. That was when she had accepted his engagement ring, however. It seemed the least she could do after all he had done for her. Back then she had thought, hoped, she would fall in love with him. It seemed so ungrateful, so foolish not to. She *wanted* to love him. And yet, somehow, that magical feeling of love had never happened. All she felt was gratitude, and guilt because she couldn't feel more.

But as Lark's quandary deepened, she was more and more tempted to marry Stanley anyway. The Cadillac was repossessed. The stores at which she had blithely purchased the feminine dresses her father loved to see her wear started sending nasty past-due notices. She discovered she didn't even own the furniture. It was mostly from stores Mr. McIntyre had smooth-talked into lending their stock to use for display purposes. In the end there was only the little compact car Lark had purchased on her own and the few dollars that were now in her purse.

The letter from her old schoolmate Beth Wyler in San Diego had been a godsend. Beth mentioned casually that her roommate had just married and moved out. Lark had telephoned Beth immediately and gotten a warm invitation to come on down. Beth was sure Lark could quite easily find some sort of secretarial or receptionist work.

And yet it was not a future which Lark could contemplate with any great degree of enthusiasm. Marrying Stanley, even if she didn't love him, would be so much easier and more secure. Lark had felt herself weakening the last time he took her to dinner. He was pleasant and attentive, the food and wine delicious, the description of the house he was buying inviting. The friends who stopped by their table obviously held Stanley in high esteem, and his status reflected a comfortable glow on Lark. It would be so easy, so *sensible* to accept the secure future Stanley offered her.

But that was when she made her decision, when she knew she must get out before it was too late. Because she didn't love him, and she knew that eventually no amount of status or home or security could make up for that lack. Sooner or later both of them would wind up bitter and miserable in a loveless marriage.

She had called Beth the very next morning and said she was on her way. She planned to sell the car as soon as she reached San Diego and use the money to tide her over until she found a job. When she was packed and ready to leave, she went by Stanley's apartment with the note and ring.

And now here she was, she thought a bit ruefully, alone on some rainswept, godforsaken road in southern Oregon, waiting for a hostile stranger to go away so she

could barge in on some acquaintances for the night.
Stanley, proper Stanley, would be horrified.

A rattle of rocks on the roof of the car startled Lark.
She peered out cautiously and drew a shaky breath of
relief as she saw it was only a scampering gray squirrel
that had dislodged the rocks. Uneasily she realized that
darkness would be upon her soon. She tapped the steering wheel, trying to decide what to do. She had assumed
the man and his pickup would have to return by this
route, but perhaps the road had some other outlet.

Finally she started the engine and eased back into the
rutted tracks of the rough road. A little farther on she
passed a prominent "No Trespassing—Violators Will Be
Prosecuted" sign which Mike and Jeanne must have
erected to keep out unwanted visitors. She hoped that
didn't include her! She drove slowly but steadily. Rank
grass growing between the ruts brushed the underside of
her car. She could see little in the growing darkness, but
she had the impression the countryside was growing ever
wilder and steeper.

Somewhere along the way she began to suspect she
was on the wrong road. Surely even Mike and Jeanne
wouldn't live all alone in this isolation. Her heart
thudded as the beam of her car lights picked up the eyes
of some wild creature glowing back at her.

Finally she had to admit the obvious. She *was* on the
wrong road. This must be just another of the abandoned
logging roads Mike and Jeanne had said crisscrossed the
countryside.

She glanced around apprehensively, searching for
someplace to turn around, but the road was too narrow
and she had to keep going. Finally, with a sigh of relief,
she saw the road widen into a sloping clearing.

She braked and looked around curiously. Obviously
her rather tardy realization that she was on the wrong
road was correct. The beam of her headlights lit up a
cluster of crumbling shacks at the edge of the clearing.
One building had recently been partially burned. The

clearing was dotted with huge stumps and pieces of rusting machinery, remnants of some long-ago logging activities. Modern cans and plastic containers and other garbage also littered the ground, incongruous and ugly in the wild setting.

It was not a scene to inspire confidence. Lark opened the window so she could see to determine the best way to turn around. She jumped when a mocking voice spoke almost in her ear.

"You decided to come up, I see. I thought you might have better sense."

Lark gasped, one hand touching her slender throat. He was standing only inches from the car, a look of sardonic amusement on his face. Behind him she now saw the dim outline of the big pickup. Evidently he had parked here and waited for her. *Why?* A jarring chill shot through her as she realized the dangers possible in this situation.

"I . . . I seem to have taken the wrong road," she stammered. "I'm sorry—"

He cut off her apology. "This is the right road. It's just that your friends aren't here anymore. I ran them off last week. I just came up this evening to make sure they hadn't sneaked back."

Lark stared at him blankly. Was the man mad? What in the world was he talking about?

"Didn't you see the 'No Trespassing' sign?" he pursued. "Or do you have the same attitude toward signs and disregard for private property that your friends have?"

"Of course I saw the sign," Lark snapped. "But since I had been invited, I presumed it didn't apply to me." Then she hesitated, remembering that she obviously was on the wrong road and probably was trespassing.

"It applies to you," he growled. "You may be a little cleaner"—he paused, giving her an appraising glance that brought a flush to her cheeks—"and considerably more attractive than most of your friends, but I'm telling you the same thing I told them. Get out and don't come back, or the next time I'll have the sheriff after you!"

He took a menacing step toward her, and Lark just stared at him, too astonished to move. "Well?" he prodded.

Lark was galvanized into action. She took her foot off the brake and stepped on the accelerator. The car shot forward, farther and faster than she intended. She jerked the gearshift into reverse and whipped backward in a circular turn, noting with a certain grim satisfaction that he had to jump to one side to avoid being hit. Her eyes were on the rearview mirror, watching him in the red glow of her taillights, when the car suddenly jolted to a stop with a grinding, grating noise from underneath. Frantically she shoved the gearshift forward again, feeling the wheels spin as the car strained to free itself from whatever was holding it.

The man walked toward her trapped car. She could see him in the rearview mirror, the shadowy shape of his powerful figure as menacing as some predator from the wilds that surrounded them. She struggled with the gearshift, alternately trying to go forward and then backward, but nothing worked. There appeared to be no obstacle ahead of her, so she knew she must have run over a large rock or stump and caught the underneath side of the car on it.

His hand was on the door when unexpectedly the car broke free and careened headlong down the road. Lark struggled to control the steering wheel as the car lurched and bounced from side to side, hitting rocks and ruts and churning up a spray of muddy dirt. One frantic glance in the mirror showed the outline of the broad-shouldered man standing there with hands on hips, astonishment apparent in every line of his body. At least she had wiped that aloof, superior expression off his face, she thought grimly.

She didn't slow down until the car whipped around a curve, and even then she drove considerably faster than she had coming up, anxious to put as much distance as possible between herself and the arrogant stranger. He hadn't even given her a chance to explain, just chased her off as if she were some sort of criminal!

She was aware before driving very far that the car was behaving peculiarly. It felt sluggish, almost as if it were dragging something. She considered stopping and checking to see if a stick or branch was caught underneath, but she didn't want to take the time. All she wanted to do now was escape before the big pickup came roaring down the road behind her. For all she knew the man could be a mugger, a murderer, or a madman, considering the strange way he had parked and waited for her.

She kept driving, but even though the road was downhill and she pressed harder and harder on the accelerator, the car didn't respond. It crept along sluggishly, while she shot frequent nervous glances at the rearview mirror, expecting any moment to find the big pickup looming menacingly behind her. Then she became aware of something else, a rattling knock coming from the engine. Resolutely she closed her ears to it. The car had been serviced only a few days before she left Seattle, and the attendant had checked oil and radiator the last time she bought gas.

Then, with the eruption of a smoky blue cloud, the engine abruptly stopped dead. Lark jiggled the ignition key, pumped the gas pedal, haphazardly pushed and pulled handles and knobs on the dashboard. Nothing happened. *Nothing.*

Now what? She found a flashlight and slid out of the car. Gingerly she lifted the hood and peered at the mechanical mystery within. Lark's knowledge of the internal workings of the automobile was practically nil. It was another of the things her father had said she shouldn't bother her "pretty head" about. But even Lark's inexperienced nose could detect something abnormal in the hot, burned odor of the engine. She tentatively wiggled wires and jiggled metallic parts, but nothing happened. Perhaps if she just waited the engine would cool off and everything would be all right, she thought hopefully.

It was then that she heard the noise that she had dreaded, the roar of the big pickup, inexorably drawing closer moment by moment as the sound vibrated across the stillness of the wild country.

Lark glanced around wildly as the full meaning of her predicament dawned on her. She was miles from any-where, with an impatient, perhaps even dangerous stranger rapidly approaching.

And she had the road blocked again.

Chapter Two

Lark had little time to speculate about what she should do. Within moments the big pickup pulled in behind her little car. She threw up a hand to shield her eyes from the blazing headlights. A voice spoke to her from behind the glare.

"I thought I'd find you stopped down here somewhere." There was a lazy superiority in his voice that Lark found infuriating, but she realized she was in no position to vent her anger.

As calmly as possible, she said, "The engine seems a little hot. I'm just letting it cool off. I'll move out of your way as soon as possible."

He stepped into the glare of the headlights and laughed, his head thrown back to reveal the husky column of his throat and even white teeth. "I think your problems are a good deal more serious than a hot engine."

He sounded maliciously amused, and Lark desperately wished she could disdainfully ignore him, but the need to find out what was wrong with her car deprived her of that pleasure. "What do you mean?"

He didn't answer. Without asking permission, he took the flashlight out of her hand. He probed the interior of the engine compartment with the beam, then slid partway under the car and flashed the beam upward. Finally he stood up, brushing bits of dirt and grass from his Levi's.

"Just what I figured," he said with that same infuriating air of superiority. "You drove over a chunk of old machinery when you threw your temper tantrum up there. It knocked a fist-sized hole in the underside of the engine. All the oil leaked out."

"Temper tantrum!" Lark gasped furiously, blue eyes blazing. "You told me to get out—as if I were some sort of criminal, I might add. I was merely trying to comply as quickly as possible!"

"An admirable effort, I'm sure," he said dryly. "However, you're still trespassing on the property." He nodded his head toward the back side of the "No Trespassing" sign revealed by the powerful beam of the pickup's headlights.

"There may be a spare can of oil in the trunk of the car," Lark said loftily, refusing to be apologetic in the face of his arrogant rudeness. His abrasive personality obviously did not match his dark good looks.

"A can of oil isn't going to do you any good," he said grimly. "Neither will six cans. Or a dozen."

"What do you mean?" Lark faltered in dismay.

"There's oil all over the road up there. Unless I miss my guess, the engine is ruined," he said flatly. "That hole is so big the oil drained out as if someone had opened a faucet on it. And when that happens, the engine freezes up tight and can't run."

"Freezes up?" Lark repeated doubtfully. "But the engine seemed hot, not cold."

In the glare of the headlights his chiseled features had an exasperated, don't-women-know-anything-about-cars look. " 'Freezing up' is merely an expression. It means that without oil to lubricate the moving parts of the engine, they tighten up and can't move. By that time the damage has been done, and adding more oil won't do any good."

The full extent of her predicament finally dawned on Lark, and her "Oh!" came out as a gasp. A ruined engine! What would that cost to repair or replace? Her thoughts were chaotic. Alone, in a strange place, with an immobilized car and little money. She didn't know how to contact Mike and Jeanne now that the map had failed her. She had no place to stay and no way to go on. She was not even certain where she was right now, except that she was in the company of a hostile stranger.

Suddenly the problems seemed overwhelming, too much to cope with. She had been through so much these last few months, and now she faced a new and desperate problem. Her shoulders sagged despairingly and she felt tears blurring her eyes. Her injured hand throbbed, and a sudden dizziness made her brace herself against the car. She hadn't eaten since breakfast, she realized vaguely, skipping lunch to save money.

"Are you all right?" he asked sharply.

"Isn't . . . isn't there something that could be done?" she asked as she looked up at him with tear-bright eyes, hands spread appealingly.

He regarded her for a moment, his expression unfathomable, but for a moment Lark thought she saw a softening of the hard eyes and sensuous mouth. Then he laughed grimly. "That's very effective. I'm sure that delicate, helpless little air of yours would have many a man practically flipping somersaults to help you."

Lark gasped. He thought she was putting on some sort of act, deliberately using feminine wiles and tears and helplessness in an effort to cajole him into helping her!

"I'm sure I don't know what you're talking about," she said icily. Cold fury dried the tears in her eyes and straightened her sagging shoulders. "I merely asked if anything could be done to repair my car, and you chose to believe that I'm throwing myself at you."

"A woman might throw herself at a man," he observed. "Little girls stand around and look pretty and helpless."

Lark gasped again. "Of all the . . . the incredible nerve!" she began. Angrily she tossed a stray strand of hair out of her eyes.

Lazily he reached out and tucked the strand of hair behind her ear. "And if looking pretty and helpless doesn't work, then she stamps her foot and tosses her hair until some gullible man smiles and says, 'You're beautiful when you're angry,' " he said mockingly.

Lark gritted her teeth and clenched her hands, fighting for composure and rejecting the electric tingle his touch sent through her. "I don't see any point in continuing this ridiculous conversation," she said crisply. "My car appears to be blocking the road, so unless you choose to help me, it appears we are both stuck here."

"Oh, so now we have threats," he jeered derisively.

He gave her a long, calculating glance, then turned on his heel and disappeared into the blackness beyond the headlights. Lark couldn't look into the lights—they were too bright—but she heard the powerful pickup engine start. She watched, puzzled, as the lights backed away from her and then angled up the slope. For a moment she couldn't understand what he was doing, and then, with a stab of dismay, she realized. The big pickup was a four-wheel-drive vehicle that sat high off the ground and was quite capable of coping with steep, rough terrain, road or no road.

With a kind of horrified fascination she heard the pickup churn up the slope and lurch past her standing helplessly below. The headlights angled crazily through the trees as the pickup careened back onto the roadway ahead of her, and the red taillights glowed back at her like ominous warning signals.

She stared after them with a sinking feeling in the pit of her stomach. He was leaving her stranded out here alone in the dark, miles from anywhere! The taillights winked out of sight around a curve and she just stood there frozen with shock and fear. Over the receding sound of the pickup engine she heard the howl of some wild animal, and an answering wail vibrated from the far side of the canyon. She clutched the car door for support, willing herself to remain calm, not dissolve into hysteria or tears. It took all her willpower not to panic and run headlong, screaming, after him. She shivered, the night air chill around her, the mists closing in like a shroud. Her mind felt frozen, incapable of thinking beyond this terrifying moment of utter, desolate aloneness.

Suddenly she was astonished to see the red taillights reappear. The pickup backed to within a few feet of her car. Her knees felt buttery with relief. Hostile and taunting as he had been, at this moment his company seemed infinitely preferable to the unknown terrors of this dark, isolated mountain road. He got out of the pickup and strode back to where she stood clutching the door handle.

"I don't suppose I can leave you out here alone," he said roughly.

"Isn't that considerate of you!" Lark retorted caustically in spite of her weak-kneed relief at his return. "Now that you've analyzed my character and thoroughly humiliated me, while proving your male superiority in the bargain, of course you're generously willing to give me a lift!"

She couldn't see his features in the dim glow of the taillights, but she knew he was scowling. "I offered you a lift the same as I would anyone else stranded out here," he said curtly. "If you don't want it, that's fine with me. I'm not into playing childish games."

He stalked back to the pickup. An angry retort rose to Lark's lips, but she bit it back before making the disastrous error of speaking her feelings aloud. She couldn't afford to match tempers or wits with him. She knew he wouldn't give her a second chance.

"Wait!" she called. "Please. I . . . I really do appreciate your offer."

He paused by the open pickup door as if undecided about giving her even this much of a second chance.

"Look, I don't know what or who you think I am," she began, "but I really am just trying to find my friends." It all came out in a rush, how her friends from Seattle had bought this land and moved down here and invited her to stop in and see them sometime, how she had followed their map but evidently gotten on the wrong road. She realized she was almost babbling, but once started, she couldn't seem to stop.

He listened without comment, and his voice was still skeptical when he asked if he could see this map. Hastily Lark ran back to the car and snatched up the scrap of paper. Feeling a little breathless, she hurried back and handed it to him.

He carried the crumpled map around to the front of the pickup, where he bent over to inspect it in the glare of the headlights. She reached across his arm, pointing to the line of the road she had followed.

"See, I came past Indian Mary Park and turned off here. I'm sure I passed that road and that turnoff . . ." She broke off suddenly as she realized that in her eagerness to make him understand she had leaned against him and her body was pressing far too intimately against his. His lean, powerful muscles seemed to burn into her body, and she jerked back, her face flaming, grateful for the protective darkness so he could not see her agitation. He turned and looked at her, and she had the awful feeling he was about to make some derisive, taunting comment about her trying to throw herself at him again. "And so, here I am," she finished hurriedly. "I'd be willing to pay you for your assistance, of course."

"All right. Get in the pickup. We'll see if we can find the place." He still sounded skeptical. "You're sure your friends *bought* this property?" he added.

She was puzzled by his emphasis, but passed it off as another of his strange peculiarities. "Why don't you ask them yourself when we find them?" she challenged.

He nodded. "I may just do that. Do you need anything out of the car?"

She dragged an overnight bag out of the car. She hated to leave her other possessions, scanty as they were, out here, but at that moment it seemed unlikely anyone would happen along to steal anything. She would get Mike and Jeanne to bring her back first thing in the morning. In spite of this man's skeptical attitude about finding her friends, there was an authoritative, capable air about him that made Lark feel certain that if anyone could find them, he could.

She climbed into the pickup on the passenger's side. They jolted along in silence. Lark surreptitiously watched him out of the corner of her eye, reluctantly curious about him. He seemed at home in workclothes and this rough pickup, but there was an indefinable air of something else about him, as if he might be equally at home in more sophisticated dress and surroundings.

"Do you work around here?" she asked.

"I'm employed by the Hammond Lodge. It's on the river, near where you turned off."

"What do you do?" she pursued.

"River guide." He shrugged. "Caretaker."

He glanced at her as if considering asking some questions of his own, but decided against it. Lark had the distinct feeling he was somehow testing her, waiting for proof that her friends and their property really existed. She was beginning to get rather annoyed with that odd attitude.

They met no cars on the lonely road. He stopped once to study the little map again, and turned off on a narrow road Lark didn't even remember seeing. A little farther on he turned again, beside a huge pine tree, and stopped abruptly.

"This is it," he stated laconically.

Lark just stared. In the beam of the headlights, half-hidden by trees and brush, she could see the little cabin with windows boarded up. Undisturbed pine needles covered the driveway, and a "For Sale" sign hung from the padlocked metal gate barring the way.

"There . . . there must be some mistake," Lark stammered in disbelief. A little desperately she added, "Maybe their place is farther on."

He shook his head and pointed to another half-hidden, weatherbeaten sign tacked to a tree with the words "Mike and Jeanne Denton" hand-carved on it. Mike, she recalled numbly, had been proud of his woodworking abilities.

She shook her head helplessly. "I just can't believe it. They had so many plans."

"Lots of people come here with unrealistic hopes and plans," he said dispassionately. "They want to get away from city life and think they can be self-supporting on a few acres of dry hillside land. When reality catches up with them and they get tired of roughing it, they pack up and move on."

Lark didn't know what to say. Her mind seemed to have stopped functioning. There was just an awful, blank sense of helplessness, of having reached a dead end.

"I'm sorry I was so rough on you back there," the man said gruffly.

The words failed to penetrate the numbness of her mind. With an effort she brought both mind and eyes to focus on him. "What?"

"I said, I'm sorry I was so rude and suspicious of you," he repeated with unnatural loudness. He sounded as if apologies did not come easily to him. Nor frequently, Lark suspected.

"I think you do owe me some sort of explanation," she said slowly. "I really was on that road by accident."

"I can see that now," he agreed grudgingly. He hesitated, obviously not accustomed to having to explain or justify his actions. "As I said, a lot of people like your friends, who dream of owning a few acres and living off the land, move into this area. I rather admire them for their ambition and energy, though, unfortunately, most of them are doomed to failure. But there's another type I haven't any use for at all." His voice hardened. "These are the ones who come in, usually in hippie-type groups, and seem to think they have the right to move in on any vacant land they see. They talk about saving the environment and getting back to nature, but what they do is chop down trees and litter the area with garbage. And usually plant a plot of marijuana to boot. I've chased two groups of them away from that old logging camp recently. But not before they almost burned down one of the old buildings. If that had happened during the summer, it would surely have started a forest fire."

His voice grew more angry as he talked, but finally he paused and smiled a little grimly.

"I get rather worked up about this particular subject, as you can see. I thought you were another one of that type, come to move in with your friends who were trespassing and littering private property."

"Perhaps you shouldn't be so quick to judge or jump to conclusions," she said lightly.

"I've offered my apologies," he reminded curtly, a trace of the familiar arrogance creeping back into his voice.

"Yes. Thank you," Lark said wearily. She was in no condition for verbal sparring matches. She had to think what to do. There was no point in going back to her car tonight. Yet it was miles back to the freeway, and she couldn't recall having seen any motels along the way. She didn't even know how far it was to the next town where rooms might be available. With a sinking heart she also remembered this was Saturday evening. Finding someone to work on her car might well be impossible until Monday morning. Then, with a glimmer of hope, she remembered this man had said he worked at a lodge nearby. She turned to him hopefully.

"Would the lodge where you work have any rooms available to rent for the night?"

He shook his head. "The lodge is closed for the season. There'll be a few guests coming early next month, but the main season for running white-water trips on the river doesn't start until later in the month, after Memorial Day."

"Oh." Lark's spirits plummeted again. She looked down at her hands, blinking back tears, determined not to let this man think she was seeking sympathy.

"However, since the lodge is empty, I don't suppose it would do any harm if you stayed there for a night or two," he said nonchalantly.

Lark's lips parted as she lifted her eyes to look at him again, hardly able to believe this bit of good fortune. She tried to keep her lips from trembling in relief.

"Oh, Mr. . . ."

"Whitcomb," he supplied. "Rand Whitcomb."

"Mr. Whitcomb, I'm so grateful. I . . ." Then she broke off abruptly.

Rand Whitcomb was leaning back against the door of the pickup, his lean body turned toward her, one leg resting casually on the seat. There was a lazy, almost speculative look on his face as his eyes traveled insolently over her slim figure, and Lark's cheeks burned as she suddenly suspected what was behind his sudden generosity. Undoubtedly, as caretaker, he slept at the lodge too.

"I'd pay the proper rate for a room, of course," she said hurriedly.

"Perhaps we should discuss just how grateful you'd be," he suggested with the same lazy, speculative look.

Lark caught her breath as the insinuation hit her. "Mr. Whitcomb—"

"Call me Rand," he cut in.

"Mr. Whitcomb, if you are suggesting that I might be willing to . . . would . . ." Words failed her in her anger. She slipped the strap of her purse over her wrist and yanked at her overnight bag. She would rather take her chances alone in the dark than with this man!

"My dear Miss . . ."

"Lark McIntyre," Lark said aloofly.

"My dear Miss McIntyre, if I were suggesting you spend the night with me, I wouldn't beat around the bush about it. I'd just ask," he snapped bluntly. "Now who's jumping to conclusions?"

She had been neatly trapped, she realized. He was looking at her disdainfully now, as if she were presumptuous even to think he might be attracted to her. Suddenly her face felt gritty after the day's travels. She became aware that her blond hair, usually bouncy and lively, drooped limply on her shoulders. Her turtleneck sweater felt sticky, and she knew her lipstick must have long since disappeared.

"I didn't mean . . . I mean . . ." she stammered lamely.

"What *do* you mean?" he asked pointedly.

"Does anyone else stay at the lodge?"

"There's Mrs. Quigley. She's the cook and head housekeeper. She stays on all winter. She's very middle-aged and mothers all the girls who work at the lodge during the season." His voice was condescending, a superior adult assuring a fearful child that the bogeyman wasn't going to get her. "And I'm not in the habit of forcing myself on an unwilling girl," he added contemptuously.

That was probably true, Lark thought grudgingly. With his dark good looks and potent masculinity, he no doubt had his pick of female companionship. She brushed that thought out of her mind and weighed the important factors. She desperately needed a place to stay for the next couple of nights. In spite of Rand Whitcomb's scorn, she still didn't quite trust his intentions, but the presence of a motherly, middle-aged chaperon would surely ensure that nothing untoward happened.

He lifted a dark eyebrow impatiently.

Lark nodded, and he expertly backed the pickup out of the driveway. They wound their way through the twists and turns that took them back to the road that followed the river. It was only a short distance from there to the lodge, which was built between the road and the river. In the glow of a big outdoor light Lark saw a rambling two-story building built of massive logs notched together and surrounded by huge cedar and oak trees. Several outbuildings and smaller cabins were scattered among the trees.

Rand pulled the pickup around to a rear entrance, giving her little time for inspection. He took her overnight case and led the way down a dimly lit hall. Through a side door Lark caught a glimpse of a gleaming modern kitchen.

He motioned with a nod of his head toward another hallway. "My room is back that way."

To Lark's relief, he did not make any move to take her bag in that direction. He led her through what appeared to be a main lobby, also too dark for much inspection, then up a flight of stairs to a hallway of closed doors. Selecting one at random, he opened the door and switched on a light. For the first time Lark noted that his clothes were dirty and mud-spattered. Guiltily she realized that this was probably a souvenir of her hasty action with the car at the logging camp.

"It's very nice," Lark said sincerely, her wariness relaxing a little. "I really appreciate your help."

"Are you hungry? We can probably whip up something in the kitchen, though Mrs. Quigley gets rather irate if anyone disturbs her domain."

"I'm starved," Lark admitted honestly.

"I'll meet you down in the kitchen in a few minutes, then," he said, setting her bag on a chair by the bed. "You'll probably want to freshen up first. Bathroom over there."

"Thank you."

"Unfortunately, the water heater for the guest rooms is turned off for the season, so you'll have to do without hot water." With a wickedly amused glint in his eyes he added, "Unless, of course, you'd care to share my facilities?"

"Thank you, I can get along quite nicely without hot water," Lark interrupted hastily.

He shrugged. "As you will."

Lark took a moment to inspect the room after the door closed behind him. The ceiling was slanting, giving the room a cozy, intimate air. The furniture was mellow pine, warm and rustic. A colorful Navajo Indian-style bedspread covered the bed, and two paintings of river scenes decorated the pine-paneled walls.

Lark looked longingly at the big tub in the bathroom, but Rand was right. There was no hot water. She settled for a hasty splash of cold water on hands and face. The overnight bag contained only one change of clothes, an old pair of beige slacks that were comfortable for traveling, and a plain white blouse. Perversely, in spite of a continuing wariness about Rand Whitcomb, Lark wished she had something more attractive to put on. She brushed her hair lightly to bring back its luster and bounce and added a touch of coppery lipstick to her mouth. She met Rand just as he was entering the kitchen below. A quick flick of his eyes told her he noted her efforts to make herself more presentable. He had showered, from the looks of his damp, crisp hair, and changed to slacks and knit shirt.

"How about bacon and eggs and toast?" he asked as he peered into the refrigerator.

"Sounds marvelous to me. Shall I cook?"

He raised a dark eyebrow. "You cook?"

"For the last few years I did practically all the cooking and housekeeping for my father and myself," she assured him.

He looked at her with a certain degree of surprise. "Perhaps you're not quite as fragile and helpless as you appear," he observed.

While they were talking, Lark expertly spread strips of bacon on the grill, located the toaster, and set out butter and strawberry jam. A small coffeepot sat beside the big commercial-type pot evidently used when guests were in residence, and she set it on to perk. Within minutes she had an attractive, delicious meal on the table.

Rand ate appreciatively. Lark was too hungry to

bother with small talk. She was on her third buttery egg and savoring a second piece of toast with thick jam before she began to lose that famished feeling.

"I skipped lunch," she said apologetically, by way of explanation for her large appetite.

"I see." He leaned back in his chair, his dark eyes appraising her again. "You're in a hurry to get somewhere?"

Lark explained briefly, without going into the reasons why, that she was on her way to room with a girlfriend in San Diego. "My problem right now, of course, is what to do about the car."

"You may be able to get it towed in tomorrow, but you won't find any repair shops open until Monday. At least, none which can handle that major a job," he said, comfirming what she had suspected earlier. Suddenly he leaned forward. "What did you do to your hand?"

Lark looked down. She had lost the makeshift handkerchief bandage, and the scratch was bleeding again.

"Let me see it," he demanded.

"It's nothing," she protested, sliding her hand under the table. "Just a scratch from a wild-blackberry bush."

"Let me see it," he repeated.

Reluctantly she held out her hand and he took it in his, turning the jagged scratch up to the light. The embedded thorns looked purplish beneath her fair skin. She was aware of a persistent ache in the hand, until now pushed into the background by her other problems. She tried to pull away, uneasy at the physical contact between them, even though he seemed quite impersonal and businesslike. Her own feelings, improbable as it seemed, were anything but businesslike, and she wondered if he felt the erratic fluttering of her pulse when he touched her.

"We'll have to get those thorns out. Otherwise they're apt to get infected and fester," he said decisively.

She murmured a protest, but he was already gone. He

returned a minute later with tweezers and antiseptic and bandages.

He reached for her hand, but she pulled back, wary of the unexpected reaction his touch aroused in her. "I'll do it myself," she said.

She took the tweezers and worked determinedly at the buried thorns, but the thorns were embedded in her right hand, so she was forced to use her left hand on the tweezers. In several minutes all she managed was to make a rather bloody mess of her hand and bring tears of pain to her eyes.

"Okay, that's enough," he said. His voice allowed for no argument. He took the tweezers in one hand, her injured hand in the other, and efficiently removed the thorns one by one. His hands were capable and thorough but not ungentle.

She studied him while he worked with his head bent intently over her hand. His dark hair was thick and heavy, the ends curling slightly where they met the back of his neck. He wasn't tan at this time of year in this climate, and yet neither was he pale. His shoulder muscles rippled under the knit shirt as he worked with incongruous delicacy on the exacting task. Somehow the fact that he was merely a caretaker at an empty lodge did not fit with the air of self-assurance and authority he possessed. Once he glanced up and caught her scrutinizing him. She flushed, embarrassed, but he merely asked if he was hurting her and she managed to murmur a no.

He finished the job by applying antiseptic, warning that it would sting, then a soothing cream, and finally a bandage. When he was finished, he put her right hand down and unexpectedly picked up the left one.

"You usually wear a ring," he commented.

Lark was surprised and flustered by the unexpected remark. The faint line left by the removed engagement ring was so slight as to be almost unnoticeable.

"You're very observant," she finally said evasively.

"Wedding ring?" He massaged the ring finger with a

casual sensuousness, and the unexpected thought touched Lark's mind that people had once believed there was a direct connection between the ring finger and the heart. From the way her own heart was suddenly hammering, she could almost believe it. "No. Engagement ring, I'd say," he decided. "Very recently removed."

She pulled her hand away and started picking up the used dishes. "I really don't think that is any of your business," she said a little breathlessly.

Without warning he grabbed her by the arm and whirled her around to face him, his other hand lifting her chin and forcing her eyes to meet his. "Perhaps I intend to make it my business," he said softly. "I get the feeling you are not so much going *to* something as running *away* from something else."

"And that, again, is none of your business," she shot back, struggling to escape from his grasp. He used a knee to pin her against the kitchen cabinets, and she was shiveringly aware of his lean male strength.

"Is that how you handle problems, by running away from them?" he asked. His grip didn't loosen and his eyes bored into hers with a disturbing intensity. There was a certain scorn in his voice as he added, "I would have thought you had more backbone than that."

"Mr. Whitcomb, you have no knowledge at all of what problems I have faced, or anything about me," Lark said, the words coming out jerky in her anger. Surprisingly, she found herself near tears. What right had he to judge her so contemptuously, to accuse her of running away? But she certainly had no intention of explaining her personal affairs to him. Realizing that further physical struggle against his superior strength was useless, she held herself motionless and rigid. "If you will take your hands off me, I'll get on with clearing the table," she said icily.

He released her and watched as she carried the dishes to the sink. She felt oddly unsteady on her feet.

"There's an automatic dishwasher," he pointed out.

"That won't be necessary. I can do these few things by hand."

"You really shouldn't get that bandage wet," he warned.

"I believe you said the housekeeper would be quite irate if she found her domain in an untidy condition." Lark efficiently wiped the grill clean.

He shrugged. "There's still no need to do the dishes tonight."

Lark turned around slowly. "What do you mean?"

"Mrs. Quigley is away for the weekend. She won't be back until Monday." His lips twitched in wicked amusement.

Lark stared at him, her hands clutching the counter behind her, her eyes wide. It was the assurance of that middle-aged, motherly presence at the lodge that had persuaded her to come here, and now he was telling her they were alone for the night in the huge, empty lodge.

"Mr. Whitcomb—" she began furiously.

"Call me Rand," he suggested lazily. "No need for formality when just the two of us are going to be spending the night here together."

Chapter Three

"You tricked me!" Lark gasped.

"Did I?" he returned with an insolent quirk of an eyebrow.

"You told me the housekeeper was here at the lodge, that the two of us wouldn't be alone here!" Lark's blue eyes blazed angrily.

"Did I?" he taunted. He leaned against the kitchen counter, arms folded against the knit shirt covering his muscular chest.

Lark's blue eyes locked in conflict with his dark ones while her mind raced back over the earlier conversation. She tried to recall exactly what it was he had said. Her eyes dropped as, reluctantly, she had to admit he was right. He had said Mrs. Quigley stayed on for the winter, that she mothered the girls who worked at the lodge during the summer. But he had not actually stated the woman would be on the premises this very night.

"You . . . you're just playing with words!" Lark sputtered. "You know you led me to believe—"

"I know you jumped to conclusions," he said blandly. There was a glint of amusement, or perhaps triumph, in his eyes as he added with a faint smile, "Not for the first time, as I seem to recall."

"You tricked me!" Lark repeated doggedly. She

34

started to toss a stray strand of hair out of her eyes, remembered his earlier taunts, and let the loose golden curl trail across her cheek.

He straightened, the air of amused tolerance with her anger suddenly hardening. "And where would you be if I hadn't 'tricked' you, as you put it?" he demanded harshly. "Stubbornly huddled under some wet tree, hungry, scared to death—"

"And probably safer than I am here!" Lark retorted. "Did it hurt your masculine ego to learn that at least one woman doesn't care to spend the night in your bed?"

"You seem somewhat preoccupied with the impression that I want to make love to you," Rand observed coolly. "It almost makes one think you protest too much, that you *want*—"

"How dare you!" Lark gasped. Angrily she reached for something, anything, to fling at him and wipe that taunting expression off his face. Her fingers curled around one of the heavy pottery mugs.

But before she could fling it at him, he closed the space between them with one lithe stride. His harsh grip on her wrist forced the cup from her nerveless fingers. She made an angry but awkward slash at his face with her left hand and then he pinioned that hand too.

"Oh, no, you don't," he muttered, imprisoning her with the hard length of his body before she could use the only weapons she had left, her feet.

She stared up at him in frustrated fury as her kick was thwarted in mid-attack. Her arms were spread helplessly on either side of her, her body arched backward against the kitchen counter by the lean, unyielding length of his muscular form.

"Perhaps we ought to find out what it is you really want," he suggested. His voice held a soft menace.

"I want you to let me go!" She twisted frantically from side to side, but she might as well have struggled against a steel trap. As if her struggles were of no consequence, he dipped his head and rained a shower of soft, fiery kisses on her face. When she flung her head to one side to avoid the sensuous assault, his head dipped lower to conquer the vulnerable curve of her throat and the exquisitely sensitive lobe of her ear, then leisurely moved back to explore the corners of her mouth.

She gave up the struggle with him because she suddenly found there was another, even more desperate struggle going on. This one was within herself, a struggle not to respond to the softly tantalizing caress of his lips, at odds with the iron grip on her wrists. She held herself rigid, desperately trying to turn off the outrageous messages her usually sensible nerves conveyed, messages that were assaulting her, awakening unfamiliar parts of her body in spite of her desperate grip on control. She could feel the hard, animal heat of his body against her own vulnerable softness, heard the sound of ragged breathing and realized it was her own.

Suddenly, as his grip moved up to her shoulders, she found her hands were free . . . but she made no move to escape. She had the bewildering feeling that if she did not clutch the counter with all her strength, her hands might betray her by creeping around his leanly muscular body.

When his hands slipped up to frame her face, she knew with a sinking certainty he was going to kiss her mouth, and just as certainly she knew that she could no longer hold herself rigidly unresponsive. His eyes stared down into hers.

"Rand . . ." she said helplessly. Abruptly he released her, and she didn't know if it was relief or disappointment that made her draw a deep, tremulous breath and then say shakily, "Well, are you satisfied? Did you really think a . . . a few kisses would send me racing to your bed?"

"I think I've had enough of your accusations that the only thing on my mind is getting you into my bed," he said grimly. "For one thing, I don't recall having invited you there, so perhaps it is *your* ego that is bruised. For another, I prefer the companionship of a willing woman to a temperamental little girl who enjoys scratching, kicking, and throwing a tantrum."

He was still standing directly in front of her, his powerful body blocking her way, but his expression was oddly bemused.

"Go up to bed," he finally said roughly.

There was a phone on the kitchen wall. Lark's glance darted to it. Perhaps she could call a cab . . .

He saw the glance and unexpectedly laughed. He reached out and tucked a stray strand of hair behind her ear. "Don't worry. You're quite safe. Something about you brings out both the predatory and protective instincts in me, but the protective has won." He paused and then added with a sardonic smile, "At least for tonight."

"How gallant of you!"

He scowled at her defiant retort, and his eyes roamed her slim body, still pressed against the kitchen counter. "But don't push me," he growled warningly. "The balance of power isn't all that heavily in favor of the protective instinct."

Lark started to snap another defiant retort, then thought better of it. She kept her eyes fixed warily on his.

He smiled again, a gleam of something Lark couldn't quite define in his eyes. One forefinger brushed her lightly under the chin. "Good night, little Miss Innocence. Sweet dreams."

Then he was gone, a mocking smile flung at her over his shoulder. It took several moments for Lark's wits to recover, and then she dashed around the room, furiously wiping up the table, washing and drying and putting away the dishes, her mind producing all the cutting remarks she should have made to him. And the worst part, the most humiliating thing of all, was that she knew he was well aware that he had aroused something new and disturbing within her. His mocking smile had said as much. Finally she switched off the light and made her way upstairs, awkwardly stumbling into two wrong rooms before locating the correct door.

Her heart was thudding furiously by the time she finally closed the proper door behind her. She stood there a moment, hands clutching the knob. She thought she heard a noise, and hastily turned the lock. She had no faith at all that Rand Whitcomb, in spite of his taunts and manifest disdain, would not try to enter her room during the night. Hurriedly she crossed the room and with determined grunts and pushes and pulls finally managed to shove the heavy dresser in front of the door.

There was no way anyone was going to get through that door into this room tonight, she thought with a grim satisfaction.

The physical exertion had warmed Lark's slim body, but as she rested, catching her breath, she realized the room was distinctly cool. Evidently the heat was also turned off in this section of the lodge until paying guests arrived. She wasted no time preparing for bed.

But in spite of her weariness, sleep did not come immediately. What was Stanley thinking by now? Guiltily she realized he was probably worrying about her. But he was sensible and rather unemotional; he would soon get over his feelings for her, she rationalized. Of greater concern to her at the moment was her own problem with the car. She could only hope Rand's assessment of its condition would prove overly pessimistic.

At the thought of the man sleeping somewhere nearby in the lodge, her anger blazed again. No matter what he said, he *had* deceived her. She had come here expecting the reassuring presence of a matronly housekeeper, and now she found herself alone in the lodge with a disturbingly attractive man she still did not trust.

An unexpected sound startled Lark, and she tensed, half-expecting the door to open in spite of her precautions, but it was only the wind brushing a branch against the window. There was another sound, too, something she couldn't quite place, indistinct, and yet vaguely menacing. But in spite of it and her general state of turmoil, she eventually slept.

That muffled roar was the first thing she heard when she woke in the morning, and she lay there in the warm bed drowsily listening to it, reluctant to step out into the cold room. Finally she forced herself to slide out, and then, in spite of the chill air, she paused to gasp over the scene visible from the window and to realize what the steady background rumble and mutter was.

She had not realized from their back-door entrance last night just how close to the river the lodge was situated. It was built almost on the edge of a precipitous drop to the rushing, turbulent water below. She watched in fascination as the water swirled around boulders strewn in its path, surged over submerged obstacles that created strange hollows and huge standing waves that seemed to be trying to climb over the underwater barriers. The noise it made was almost like a live thing, an angry growl, a warning mutter.

Even below the churning rapids, where the foaming white water gave way to a stretch of calmer green water, she could see swirls and eddies, moving whirlpools that came and went, giving evidence of the hidden power of the river beneath. It was not, she thought a little shakily, like the silent, placid stream in Kansas where she often swam as a child when her mother was still alive. She felt an unexpected surge of respect for Rand's ability to challenge and conquer those turbulent waters. She shivered, realized she was standing there getting goose bumps in her flimsy nightie, and hurriedly washed and dressed.

She then had to push and pull and shove to remove the heavy dresser from where she had placed it in front of the door the night before. In broad daylight she felt a little foolish that she had thought Rand might force his way into the room. After all, he had made it quite plain that he found her too young and innocent for his experienced tastes.

At the top of the lushly carpeted stairs she paused to inspect the big combination lobby and living room below. It was rustic and comfortable-looking, with sofas and deep chairs arranged in conversational groupings around the huge rock fireplace that dominated the room. The walls were paneled in walnut. Huge windows looking out on a redwood deck flooded the room with light. Pots of luxuriant Boston ferns suspended by heavy macrame holders hung near the windows. Over the fireplace hung a massive set of polished horns flanked by a pair of large antique guns. On another wall hung a heavy Navajo rug with a bold turquoise-and-brown geometric design woven in.

Everything was on such a huge, almost grand scale that Lark felt a little breathless, as if she had stumbled into a place where everything was larger than life.

The feeling was intensified as Rand suddenly appeared in the hallway leading to the kitchen, his rugged, broad-shouldered figure almost filling the doorway. He was wearing a clean pair of Levi's and a heavy red-and-black woolen shirt, rough and masculine-looking. His dark eyes appraised her with a faintly cynical expression, but with him came the inviting fragrance of freshly perked coffee.

"That coffee smells delicious," Lark said, annoyed that her voice sounded unsteady. Her fingers trembled against the heavy railing, and she gripped the polished wood to stop them. She couldn't understand what was the matter with her, why simply seeing this man standing in the doorway below should so unnerve her. She had generally found men quite willing to do her bidding, and not at all intimidating. But Rand Whitcomb, as he had proved last night, was different from other men and certainly not susceptible to feminine wiles. At least not hers.

She walked down the steps slowly, reluctant to reach

the doorway while he still filled it. But he didn't move, merely lifted a dark eyebrow as she approached.

"Did you have a good night's sleep?" he inquired.

"Yes. I appreciate your hospitality."

"I hope the room wasn't too cold for you. I forgot to mention that the heat was turned off up there." His lips twitched in amusement. "My room is heated, of course, but you made it rather plain—"

"I was quite comfortable, thank you," Lark cut in aloofly.

She had reached the doorway now, and he deliberately raised an arm, blocking her way. Angrily she wondered if he intended to make her ask permission to pass through to the kitchen.

"Hungry?" he questioned lazily.

"Yes, as a matter of fact, I am," she admitted.

"Not surprising," he commented. "You should have worked up quite an appetite moving furniture around."

Lark's face flamed as she realized he knew she had blockaded the door. The action seemed more than a little ridiculous now, as if she had attributed to herself some sexual attractiveness which drove men wild.

He laughed and removed his arm, quite aware that he had embarrassed and humiliated her. He stepped back, motioning her toward the kitchen. She passed by him warily.

"I thought about bringing you breakfast in bed, but I had the feeling you would consider that a bit improper."

"I can fix my own breakfast, thank you," she said coolly.

He shrugged and took a seat at the table, casually tipping the chair back on two legs as he sipped his coffee and watched her. His plate showed he had already eaten. She stirred the pancake batter he had prepared and tested the griddle with a drop of water, waiting until the water sputtered and danced to indicate the temperature was right. Carefully she ladled dollops of batter onto the griddle, uncomfortably aware of his eyes watching her.

"Very good," he commented. "Too many people try to cook pancakes on an underheated griddle."

She had expected some sort of taunt from him, and the unexpectedly approving comment flustered her so that she made a sloppy job of turning the pancakes and wound up overlapping them.

"And you're an expert on pancakes, as you are on everything, no doubt," she snapped, angry both at her own clumsiness and at him for flustering her.

"I'll never starve just because I don't have some woman to cook for me," he agreed. He nodded toward the back of the stove. "There's ham already cooked."

"Thank you."

Lark dished up the pancakes and ham, seating herself as far away from him as possible at the table. He pushed butter and syrup toward her. She tried not to eat too ravenously, aware of his taunts about having worked up an appetite moving furniture.

"I plan to make some telephone calls immediately after breakfast to see about having my car repaired," she said briskly between bites. "Could you suggest a reliable repair shop?"

"The R and D Garage is about the best in town, but you won't find them open today." He regarded her thoughtfully. "Your first problem is going to be getting the car *to* a repair shop. I hope you're prepared to spend some time and money," he added pessimistically.

Lark's heart sank, but she determinedly tried not to let it show. She had neither time nor money to spare. It was imperative that she get to San Diego and find a job as quickly as possible, before her meager funds ran out.

There was a telephone in a corner of the kitchen with a directory dangling from it on a chain. Lark waited until Rand left the kitchen and then looked up the R and D Garage. He was right. There was no answer. Determinedly she went through the Yellow Pages and called several other repair shops, with equally unsuccessful results. Feeling frustrated, she remembered Rand's admonition that she must first get the car towed to a repair shop.

To her surprise, a male voice actually answered when she dialed a number listing tow-truck service. He listened in silence while she explained her problem, then said he supposed they could tow the car in today. Where was it?

In dismay Lark realized she hadn't the slightest idea how to give anyone directions to the car's location. She lamely explained that she would have to have someone else call in with that information.

She immediately went outside, looking for Rand. Last night's rain had stopped but the sky was still a leaden gray and the air distinctly cool and damp. She hurried around the grounds, past an empty swimming pool and wet tennis courts and a small playground with slides and swings for children.

She finally found Rand in a large open building where a number of sharply pointed aluminum boats were stored, plus what appeared to be some large deflated rubber rafts. Rand was working on an inflated yellow-and-black raft, carefully applying a patch to a jagged tear.

"I called about a tow truck, but I couldn't give them directions to the car," Lark said. "I was wondering if you would call them back and tell them where it's located."

"Certainly," he agreed pleasantly.

But if she had expected him to drop everything and rush in and make the telephone call to accommodate her, she was mistaken. He continued working, carefully checking the rubber raft for further damage. She walked around restlessly, inspecting some metal frameworks leaning against a wall. They had oarlocks and evidently fit on the inflated rafts. In a corner was a stack of bulky orange-and-black vests which she recognized as life jackets. On another wall hung a row of what seemed unusually long oars.

But at the moment none of this really interested her.

All she wanted was to get her car towed in so a repair shop could examine it first thing in the morning. She wrapped her arms around her body, trying to keep warm.

"You should have worn a jacket," Rand remarked.

"I didn't realize I'd have to stand around and wait. Is this going to take you long?" she asked impatiently.

"I still have to inflate and inspect those rafts over there." He gave her a glance that suggested that if she knew what was good for her she had better not try to hurry him. "There's a jacket hanging over by the oars."

She started to snap that she didn't want the jacket, but thought better of it and instead walked over and took the heavy jacket off its hook. It was several sizes too large for her, but she wrapped it around her shoulders, grudgingly grateful for its protective warmth.

She leaned against the stacked aluminum boats, trying to quell her impatience. "Have you been a river guide long?" she asked.

"I started working for the lodge in mid-season last summer. But I've been running the river ever since I was old enough to handle a pair of oars."

"Wouldn't using a motor be easier?"

"The lodge runs some jet boat trips on this part of the river, but the trips I guide are white-water runs through the area of the river designated as wild and scenic by the federal government. No motorized craft allowed there," he explained.

In spite of her impatience, Lark found herself interested both in the man and in the river. "What did you do before you came to work at the lodge?" she asked curiously.

He shrugged. "Logging."

He looked the part of a logger, with his rugged physique and rough clothing, and yet there was that air of self-assured sophistication about him that somehow didn't fit with river guide or caretaker or logger. Lark wanted to ask more questions, but he didn't give her the chance, deftly turning the conversation away from himself.

"How about you?" he asked. "What did you do before you took to wandering around on strange mountain roads?"

"You make me sound irresponsible and incompetent!" Lark said heatedly. "I thought you understood I had simply made a mistake."

"I still get the impression you're running away from something." He looked up suddenly, his dark eyes appraising her as if they could reach into her very mind; then turned his attention back to the raft, running sensitive fingers over the D-rings attached to the sides, checking to make sure they were secure. "Perhaps from the donor of the ring that was recently on your finger?"

When Lark didn't reply, he glanced at her again. "What did he do? Beat you? Chase around with other women? Drink?"

"Don't be ridiculous," Lark scoffed. The very idea of sober, staid Stanley doing any of those things was so preposterous that under different circumstances Lark would have laughed. Now she felt only an angry annoyance at this prying into her private affairs.

"Then why *are* you running away?" he pursued bluntly. "Because you are, you know. A girl of your . . . ummm . . . type doesn't usually take off in an old car with meager funds without some very good reasons."

Reluctantly Lark explained about the disastrous housing-development project and her father's death. "I stayed and did all I possibly could," she said defensively, her lower lip unexpectedly quivering as she recalled the days and nights of abusive phone calls and her desperate attempts to pay back the losses people had suffered buying the homes. "And I didn't run away from any of it. There just wasn't any more I could do. A lawyer is winding up the details now."

He stopped working and leaned against the big raft, one foot crossed over the other, arms folded. "And so

we come back to . . . What was his name? Stanley.
You're sure he had nothing to do with your leaving?"

"Perhaps a little," she admitted reluctantly.

"Did he break the engagement and ask for his ring
back?" Rand asked.

"I really don't think that is any of your business!"
Lark flared. She walked away from the stack of aluminum boats, wishing this conversation had never gotten
started. "But if you must know, I broke the engagement," she added finally.

That information was not enough to satisfy him.
"Why?" he asked bluntly.

Lark turned and looked at him uneasily, disturbed by
the probing questions that seemed motivated by more
than mere idle speculation. Instinctively she knew Rand
Whitcomb was not a man given to gossipy curiosity. If
he were, she might have been able to stand by her statement that this was none of his business. But there was
something about his steady, probing gaze that forced her
to go on and try to explain and justify her impetuous decision and actions.

"I simply decided I didn't want to . . . *couldn't* marry
him," she said slowly.

"Why?"

"Because I don't love him!"

"But you accepted his ring and said you would marry
him at one time." His voice was like a knife, impaling
her against a wall of guilt.

"Yes, I did," she admitted, avoiding his eyes. "But it
was only because . . . because I was grateful for all he
had done to help me."

"And so you express your gratitude and thanks by
pretending to love him, accepting his ring under false
pretenses."

"No, it wasn't like that!" Lark cried, distraught blue
eyes rising to meet his. It sounded so ugly the way he
said it. "I thought . . . I mean, I hoped I could fall in
love with him. I tried! But I . . . I just don't love him.

So I decided the best thing would be for me to go away."

"I see. And what was Stanley's reaction to this sudden revelation?"

Lark's eyes dropped again. She toyed nervously with the rope fastened to the front end of the big raft. "I don't know," she admitted reluctantly.

"You *don't know?*"

"I . . . I didn't tell him in person. I just left the ring and a note in his apartment."

The words hung there, incriminating her. Defensively she tried to explain that she thought this way was better than some unpleasant, hurtful scene. Rand just listened in stony silence, and finally Lark's explanation trailed off lamely.

"What you're really saying is that you wanted to make it easy for yourself," he said contemptuously. "That you run out on unpleasant problems rather than stand and face them."

"That isn't true," she said angrily. "I told you how I stayed and took care of the subdivision problems as best I could, and that certainly wasn't pleasant."

"But that was not a problem of your making. It was more or less thrust upon you," Rand observed. "The situation with Stanley was different, and you *did* run out on the problem."

"Very well, I ran out!" Lark cried, her blue eyes bright with near-tears. "Does that satisfy you? Now, please, can't we discuss something other than my shortcomings? I . . . I'm interested in the boats."

He shrugged and walked over to the stacked aluminum boats. "These are drift boats. The earlier ones were made of wood, but most are aluminum now. As you can see, the bow is sharply pointed and upswept, and the stern is almost pointed. The boats were designed for running white-water rapids, and up until a few years ago were the type of craft most often used to run the river.

Now the inflatable rafts have more or less taken over. They can carry more passengers."

Lark was infinitely grateful that he had decided to veer away from the subject of her personal problems, and she quickly encouraged him with questions. In addition, she found herself truly interested, amazed that anyone ventured out on that turbulent, angry river seen from her window.

"Why do you still have the drift boats, then?" she asked curiously.

"The inflatable rafts are less satisfactory for fishing," he explained. "We still use the drift boats for the fall fishing trips the lodge offers."

Rand went on to explain that during the summer season the lodge offered two guided white-water trips per week. One was a four-day camping trip on which guests ate food cooked over an outdoor fire and slept in sleeping bags under the stars. The other was a three-day trip during which guests stayed overnight in remote lodges along the river. There was no way to return up the river, and guests and rafts were met at the far end of the trip and transported by car back to the lodge.

"If you weren't in such a hurry to get to San Diego, you might enjoy a river trip yourself," he suggested casually.

The idea sounded intriguing, but Lark knew she had neither the time nor the money for such an adventure. She walked over to the big yellow-and-black raft he had been patching and tapped the smooth, taut surface. The inflated raft, like the drift boats, was upswept on both ends. "What if it's punctured by a rock or stick?" she asked doubtfully. "Won't the whole thing just go *whoosh* like a burst balloon and dump everyone in the river?"

He laughed, his head thrown back to reveal the solid column of his throat. It was a warm, husky sound, unlike his humorless, derisive laughter of the night before. Unexpectedly, Lark caught herself wondering if there were other sides to this man that he had not revealed to her. So far, he had varied from unfriendly and arrogant only to taunting and accusing, but that husky laughter hinted that somewhere there was perhaps a warm, companionable side to his character. Perhaps even a loving side, she thought with an unexplainably tremulous feeling.

"The nylon and neoprene material is quite tough, and it's rare that we get any serious punctures," he said. "But you needn't fear that the raft will go *whoosh* even if it is punctured."

He showed her how the rafts were constructed in several compartments, so that if one was accidentally punctured and deflated, the others would still keep the craft afloat. "Passengers always wear life jackets through the rough rapids," he added, "and we've never yet spilled anyone into the river on any of my guided trips."

"Perhaps the river isn't as dangerous as it looks, then," she suggested. She glanced downriver at a broad stretch of calm water, which from here looked no more dangerous than a swimming pool. "In fact, some of it doesn't even look dangerous."

"And that kind of thinking is the mistake that has cost more than a few people their lives," he said grimly. "Do you know the name of the river?"

She shook her head. "No."

"It's the Rogue. A fitting name, because it's a deceptive, treacherous, unpredictable river. Any number of people get by safely doing foolish, inexperienced things while boating or swimming. But then, without warning, the river strikes and drags someone under. Never underestimate the Rogue," he added warningly.

In the background, Lark noted again the dull roar of the rapids beneath her window, and unexpectedly she shivered. "You make the river sound as if it has a mind of its own."

"Sometimes it seems as if it does," he agreed. "It changes moods like a woman. One minute it's gentle and caressing, but the next it's wild and ruthless and scratching your eyes out."

His voice was low and intense, as if remembering, and Lark wondered suddenly if it was really the river he was thinking about. She swallowed uneasily, but her voice was tart when she commented, "You must have known some rather temperamental women."

He was looking toward the river with a faraway expression on his face. With sudden intuition Lark realized that while he had no illusions about the treacherous river, he fully respected and perhaps even loved it for its wild beauty. Was that his preference in women also—wild and beautiful?

He looked back at her suddenly, a wickedly amused glint in his eyes as he considered what she had just said. "Perhaps," he finally agreed noncommittally.

Lark suddenly felt very dowdy and plain in her old beige slacks and the shapeless jacket, a far cry from the lush, wild beauty he no doubt found attractive in a woman. She shivered in spite of the heavy jacket. "I think I'll go back inside." She hesitated and then added in a carefully neutral tone, neither begging nor demanding, "I'd appreciate it very much if you would call the man with the tow truck for me."

To her surprise, Rand nonchalantly shrugged and motioned her toward a lodge door marked with a sign that read "Office." While Rand dialed the garage number, Lark inspected the wall of color photographs next to the reception desk.

Some of the photographs were of fishermen with their catch, but it was the action photographs of the rafts in white-water rapids that astonished and fascinated Lark. In one photograph the raft was tipped downward at a precarious angle, the bow lost in the surging waters. In another, white water almost obliterated boat and passengers alike. Another showed a raft slipping between the riverbank and a boulder, the space so narrow the boatman had to hold up his oars to keep from dragging on either side. Yet another showed a raft in water rampaging through boulders so thick and numerous it hardly seemed possible there was a passageway.

Lark soon realized that her flippant remark about the river not being so dangerous after all only showed her complete ignorance, that an inexperienced amateur might well not come through those wild rapids alive. And yet she had no doubt about Rand's ability to navigate the river safely. His remark that no boat or raft had ever spilled on his guided trips had not been bragging, merely a quiet statement of fact.

Then another picture drew Lark's eye, and she caught her breath as she recognized the man in it: a younger, smiling, less cynical-looking Rand. He was standing on a gently sloping grassy bank, the river and some sort of sleek, expensive racing boat in the background. He was holding one handle of a huge trophy.

Holding the other handle of the trophy was a beautiful girl, a mass of dark hair tumbling around her bare shoulders and a full, sensuous mouth smiling provocatively up at Rand. A banner of some sort was draped across her lush figure. She was more than beautiful, Lark thought with a peculiar pang somewhere deep inside her. There was an aura of vibrant sensuality about the girl, a provocative thrust of her full breasts that was somehow both challenging and promising, a wild, untamed beauty that obviously was not lost on the handsome young man at her side.

Chapter Four

Lark stared aghast at the stocky mechanic wiping his hands on a greasy rag. Rand's pessimistic predictions were more than fulfilled. The mechanic had just told her that the car needed a complete new engine, and it would take at least a week, possibly two, to order and then install one. And the cost Lark found positively staggering. It was almost as much as she had paid for the entire car!

"I just can't believe it!" Lark gasped. "Are you sure? I mean, that's so much money!"

"Lady, for anyone else it would cost more than that," the mechanic declared. "I'm only offering to do it at that price because you're a friend of my old fishing buddy here. Hey, Rand, you remember those steelhead we caught down near Hellsgate six or seven years ago?"

Rand nodded. "And your wife cooked up a big one for us, along with homemade biscuits and apple pie."

The mechanic beamed at Rand's accurate memory, but Lark just glared furiously at both of them. Here she was faced with an almost insurmountable problem and they were reminiscing about old fishing trips!

Lark chewed on her lower lip, unable to think what to do next. The cost to repair the car was far more than she had in her purse. She could hardly expect Rand to extend the hospitality of the lodge for a week or more. She could take a bus to San Diego, but without the car to sell there, she would have no funds to tide her over until she found a job.

"If it isn't too much trouble," Lark icily interrupted the fishing talk, "I'd like to discuss what to do about my car."

The mechanic shrugged. "I'd better warn you that you might just be throwing good money after bad. The clutch is in pretty poor shape, and the brakes are only fair."

Lark gasped at this fresh bad news. She looked at Rand appealingly, but his face was impassive, and angrily she realized she should have known better than to look to him for help. She was probably fortunate he hadn't chosen to make some derisive remark about her looking appealing and helpless in order to get the mechanic to bring his price down.

Finally she said uncertainly to the mechanic, "Could you perhaps keep the car while I decide what to do? I'm a little low on funds right now."

"I'd like to help you out, but I just don't have the space," the mechanic said, motioning around his crowded shop. "Tell you what I might do, though. My boy has been looking for an old junker to buy and fix up, and this one has so many things wrong with it that he ought to be a real mechanic by the time he gets done." He named a price so low that Lark gasped again. "I'm offering more than a junkyard will pay, and they're the only ones who'll buy it in its present condition."

His voice sounded sympathetic but not particularly concerned, and angrily Lark realized the men were about to start talking about fishing again.

"May I talk to you alone for a minute?" she asked Rand sharply.

He shrugged and excused himself, following Lark a few feet away while the mechanic returned to his work.

"I think your friend is some sort of crook," she stormed in an angry whisper. "First he wants a fortune to repair the car, and then he practically wants to steal it!"

Rand looked down at her, dark eyes narrowing. "I'll overlook that remark about Roger's honesty this time, because I know you're overwrought—"

"I am not *overwrought!*" Lark cut in furiously. "I simply do not care to be cheated by some small-town con man! What does he do, give you a cut off the profits on any unsuspecting customer you bring him?"

Lark was immediately aware that she had gone too far, and was just as immediately aware that her accusation was quite ridiculous. Rand's lips tightened as he looked down at her, his eyes hard and hostile and decidedly dangerous.

"I'm sorry," Lark apologized uneasily, taking a wary step backward. "That was uncalled-for."

Rand gave no indication that he accepted the apology. "So what have you decided to do?" he asked coldly.

Lark could feel tears of frustration welling up, and she turned away, determined not to let him know how totally lost and alone she felt. He would only think she was trying to play on his sympathies or use feminine wiles on him again. "I don't know," she said finally, her voice muffled.

"I have a suggestion, if you'd care to listen."

Lark turned to look up at him doubtfully. His voice was brisk and businesslike. A car pulled into the shop, and Rand touched her elbow, steering her to one side to make room for the car. In spite of her mental turmoil over her car problems, she felt her arm tingle under his touch.

"I'm listening," she said finally, her voice annoyingly tremulous and her feelings confused by her unfamiliar reaction to a mere touch. She had never felt that way when Stanley touched her. If she had, she thought ruefully, she might not be in the predicament she was in right now.

"I believe that the girls who worked at the lodge last year are returning again this year, but Mrs. Quigley needs someone on a temporary basis to help get things ready before the Hammonds return in a few days. She might be persuaded to hire you."

"Do you really think so?" Lark asked, hopes rising.

"It would be hard work, and I don't suppose the pay is much," Rand warned. "But room and board are included, of course."

Lark calculated quickly. With what the mechanic offered for her car, and if she saved everything she earned, she just might be able to get on her financial feet again.

She accepted the mechanic's offer for the car, and the deal was quickly concluded. Lark signed over the title and the mechanic handed her a few well-worn bills. She emptied the car of her possessions.

"We'll have to get together and go fishing this fall," the mechanic called to Rand as he and Lark climbed back into the big pickup. Rand waved and nodded agreement.

Lark tucked the money far back in a pocket of her purse with her other meager savings. She had an oddly lost and abandoned feeling as they drove away. The car wasn't much, but it had been her last link with the past. Now it was gone, and she had no real assurance that the so-far-unseen Mrs. Quigley would hire her.

Rand was silent on the drive back to the lodge, obviously not given to small talk. She glanced at his strong profile out of the corner of her eye, wondering why he had suggested the job. Somehow she doubted that it was a purely altruistic gesture, and it certainly couldn't be because her precarious situation had touched him. She had the feeling that he could be as hardhearted as stone, and that more than one woman had found this out to her sorrow. And yet he had suggested she stay. . . .

The thought lingered in her mind that possibly, just *possibly* he had some personal interest in her in spite of his professed disdain for her youth and innocence. But that thought was quickly quashed when they reached the lodge and Rand introduced her to Mrs. Quigley.

Mrs. Quigley was in the kitchen just finishing up a huge batch of chocolate-chip cookies. Lark, puzzled, couldn't imagine, with no guests in residence, just who was going to eat all those cookies. Mrs. Quigley was indeed large and matronly-looking, with gray hair of an independent nature and a no-nonsense expression.

"I didn't realize you would find a helper for me so soon," Mrs. Quigley remarked to Rand. Her voice held a sort of sour joviality as she added, "But then, you seem to have an inexhaustible supply of attractive young ladies."

Mrs. Quigley walked around Lark, inspecting her as if she were some sort of beast of burden and finding her none too satisfactory. "But I should have known you'd pick one on her looks and not on her abilities or experience," Mrs. Quigley sniffed, talking to Rand as if Lark were unable to hear or understand. "She looks a little delicate for all the cleaning and scrubbing that needs to be done before the Hammonds get back."

"I'm really much stronger and sturdier than I look," Lark offered.

"Any experience?" Mrs. Quigley snapped.

"I cleaned and cooked and washed and kept house for my father for years," Lark explained. "I was only twelve when my mother died, so I had to learn to do everything myself. My father is dead now too. He was killed a few months ago in a car accident." Unexpectedly Lark's voice cracked as she mentioned her father's death. She cleared her throat to go on, but Mrs. Quigley didn't give her a chance.

"Ah, you poor little thing," she said sympathetically. "You've been through enough for someone twice your age and size. You stay here awhile and we'll put some meat on your bones and take those shadows out from under your eyes."

Mrs. Quigley's sharp, aggressive manner had melted on the spot, revealing that her hard exterior was just a phony front. Lark glanced over Mrs. Quigley's shoulder at Rand, who was watching with a knowing, cynical look on his face. Furiously Lark realized he was thinking that she had manipulated Mrs. Quigley with a sad story and deliberately played on her sympathies. Just as plainly his face said he was onto her game and he certainly would not fall for her beguiling tactics.

That wasn't fair, Lark thought, her eyes meeting his angrily. She had told Mrs. Quigley nothing but the truth, and she *was* sturdier and stronger than her rather fragile appearance indicated. And she would show Rand Whitcomb she could certainly do any job that needed to be done here.

Rand stepped forward. "Do I understand that you're hiring Miss McIntyre, then?" he asked briskly.

"Yes. And what are you just standing around for? Bring her things in."

Lark was thankful that Rand didn't choose to explain that some of her things were already in the lodge because she had spent the last two nights there.

Mrs. Quigley led Lark to the dorm room where female employees, except herself, were housed. The small room had stacked bunk beds, enough for four occupants. There was a long, horizontal mirror on one wall, beneath it a wide plastic shelf and four chairs, evidently for use as a communal dressing table. A curtained closet and a small bathroom completed the quarters. It was not nearly as elegantly rustic as the upstairs guest room, but comfortable enough, and at the moment Lark was grateful for any warm shelter. Mrs. Quigley explained that there was a similar dormitory room for young men employees down the hall. Only she and Rand had private rooms.

Rand arrived carrying her boxes and luggage from the car, and a little later Lark quietly brought her overnight case down from the guest room upstairs.

That evening she telephoned long distance to Beth in San Diego and explained her disaster with the car and her acceptance of the temporary job at the lodge. She also asked Beth to forward any mail that might arrive for her there. She had not given Stanley the address in San Diego, but reluctantly she had decided she must let the lawyer who had handled her business problems and her father's estate know where he could reach her. Now Beth assured her that she would send along anything that came for her.

Lark's work began the very next morning, and as she saw the list of chores Mrs. Quigley had lined up for her, she realized she was going to need all that strength and sturdiness she had claimed to possess. All the bathrooms were to be scrubbed until they gleamed, woodwork washed, furniture polished, rugs vacuumed. Nothing was really dirty as far as Lark could tell, but Mrs. Quigley was determined that any trace of dust or grime that had accumulated during the winter must be removed.

Lark set about the work determinedly, pausing only for a lunch break at noon, then going back to work again. She saw little of Rand except at mealtimes. She was so weary she fell into bed at an almost embarrassingly early hour in the evening, but she was determined to prove to Rand she could handle the job competently without getting by on an appealing air or sad story. On the third day of her hardworking routine she was surprised by a midmorning interruption from Mrs. Quigley. She arrived bearing a cup of coffee and a fragrant piece of freshly baked banana cake.

"My goodness, child, you don't have to do everything at once," Mrs. Quigley scolded gently. "You're working too hard. Take a break now."

Lark removed the red bandanna from her hair and

wiped her sleeve across her dust-streaked face. She had been cleaning closets, right up to the last cobweb in the top corners.

"That smells delicious," she said, accepting the snack gratefully. She felt as if she had been eating like the proverbial horse the last few days, but the hard work and invigorating air seemed to keep her ravenous. After the first melting bite of banana cake she remarked sincerely that it was the best she had ever tasted.

Mrs. Quigley beamed. "During the winter I do most of the baking for the river trips," she explained. "I bake up cookies and brownies and cake and freeze them. They thaw out on the trips and come out nice and fresh and tasty."

So that explained the enormous batch of chocolate-chip cookies she had been making, Lark realized. Mrs. Quigley went on to explain that the guides cooked on the camping trips, but as much preparation as possible was done beforehand in the lodge kitchen.

"Rand cooks for guests?" Lark questioned, a little surprised in spite of his earlier assurances that he wouldn't starve without a woman around to do for him. When Mrs. Quigley nodded, Lark hesitated and finally said tentatively, "Somehow Rand doesn't really seem to . . . to belong here. I don't mean to imply it's beneath him or anything like that. It's just that . . ." Her voice trailed off awkwardly as she found it difficult to explain exactly what it was she meant.

Mrs. Quigley pursed her lips. "How did you happen to meet Rand?" she asked unexpectedly.

Lark explained about her misadventure in wandering onto the lodge property up in the mountains and how Rand had first ordered her off the property and then, albeit reluctantly, rescued her.

"The Hammonds don't own any property up that way," Mrs. Quigley said flatly. "There's just the acreage around the lodge here."

"I don't understand," Lark said, surprised. "Rand was so disturbed because some people had been living illegally on the property, and then he was absolutely furious when he thought I was coming to join them."

Mrs. Quigley laughed. She settled her comfortable bulk into the room's single easy chair while Lark perched on the edge of the bed. "Rand fusses and fumes and says he 'doesn't give a damn' about the timber company anymore, but I'd say that isn't quite true if he's still concerned about people trespassing on company property." She nodded knowingly.

Lark looked at the older woman blankly, the words making no sense to her. Mrs. Quigley noticed the look.

"What did Rand tell you about himself?" she questioned suddenly.

Haltingly Lark gathered up the few bits of information Rand had revealed. Then her coffee grew cold in the cup as Mrs. Quigley went on to tell her a great deal Rand had not revealed.

"Rand's grandfather owns the biggest timber and lumber company in the area, Robertson Timber. They own acres and acres of timberland and lumber mills and plywood mills and heaven only knows what else. Rand is part owner too, though he isn't one to talk much about such things. He has a big home in town, just standing there empty now, I suppose. Needs a wife and a passel of kids to fill it up, if you ask me. I'll bet his grandfather thinks so too. Anyway, up until last summer, Rand was general manager over everything for the company, but then he and the old man got in some big squabble over how to run things, and Rand walked out." Mrs. Quigley paused, her eyes suddenly speculative. "Or maybe the old man threw him out. Who knows? In any case, Rand has been working here at the lodge for the Hammonds since last summer."

Lark had suspected from the very beginning that there was more to Rand than he let on, but never something like this. She wondered now why he had been so silent on the subject, simply answering her question about what he had done before working at the lodge with a laconic "logging." Perhaps because he really was no longer concerned with the company? But as Mrs. Quigley had pointed out, his protective attitude about timber-company land hardly signified a lack of concern.

"Who runs the company now?" Lark asked curiously.

Mrs. Quigley shrugged. "The old man, I suppose. Old Dan Robertson himself, a tyrant if there ever was one, and I ought to know. I cooked for him years ago. I understand his health isn't too good anymore, and I doubt that his temper has improved."

Like grandfather, like grandson, Lark thought wryly, remembering Rand's fury at her trespass on company land. Then Mrs. Quigley, in a talkative mood, went on to add further information. Old Dan Robertson had had only one child, a daughter. He disapproved of her marriage to an easterner named Landon Whitcomb and said if Whitcomb wanted to work in the company he'd have to start at the bottom and work his way up.

"Landon tried, I guess, but he was killed in a logging accident when Rand was only a few years old. I guess that taught the old man a lesson, though, because Rand always had the best of everything, university education and all. And when he came out with one of those fancy degrees the old man set him up managing things right away. He didn't start at the bottom."

"But I remember Rand telling me he'd been running the river ever since he was old enough to hold a pair of oars," Lark interjected.

Mrs. Quigley laughed delightedly. "That's right. The old man had all these big plans for Rand, but Rand was always down on the river fishing or running the rapids. Had kind of a wild streak, he did. Liked fast boats, fast cars, any kind of danger and excitement. I don't suppose he told you he's run the Salmon River and the Snake. And the Colorado too. All the big, wild ones."

Lark shook her head, a little stunned by all this.

"I don't think Rand's mother ever quite forgave the old man," Mrs. Quigley added reflectively. "She blamed him for her husband's death. 'Course, she's married again now and living down in California somewhere."

The story seemed over, and Lark finished up the crumbs of her banana cake, preparing to get back to work. But Mrs. Quigley didn't move, and her gaze on Lark was thoughtful.

"You're not falling in love with him, are you?" she asked suspiciously.

"With Rand? Why, of course not!" Lark denied heatedly. That unfamiliar reaction he aroused within her might be disturbing, but it certainly had nothing to do with *love*. "He's been very helpful, but I hardly know him."

The protest came quickly, almost too quickly, and Mrs. Quigley scowled as if noting that point.

"Well, don't," she warned with surprising forcefulness. "I don't suppose he bothered to tell you about Gloria Hammond either, did he?"

Lark was halfway to the bathroom, where she intended to dump the dregs of her cold coffee, but she stopped short and turned. "No. No, he didn't," she said slowly. Suddenly she remembered the wildly beautiful girl holding the trophy with Rand in the photo. "Is she the girl in the picture with him down in the office?"

"That's her." Mrs. Quigley nodded, her lined face grimacing slightly with disapproval. "She was queen of the boat races or some fool thing that year. She was always queen of this or princess of that." She sniffed. "Always acts as if she's some sort of royalty, too, like everyone should bow down when she passes by."

"I can't quite imagine Rand bowing down to anyone," Lark said lightly.

Mrs. Quigley laughed and nodded, shifting her bulky shape in the chair. "Rand may be her match, all right." She paused. "And then again, maybe not."

"What do you mean?"

"Everybody thought Rand and Gloria were going to get married, but all of a sudden Gloria up and eloped with one of the lodge guests, some young businessman from San Francisco."

Lark was astonished at the unexpected surge of relief that flooded through her. She realized she had been gripping the coffee cup so tightly her hand was cramped. She went into the bathroom and emptied and rinsed out the cup. "Then Gloria is married now," she remarked casually.

"*Was* married," Mrs. Quigley corrected. "She was just divorced, and she'll be returning to the lodge with her parents in a few days."

Lark was glad she was out of Mrs. Quigley's sight, because she knew that shrewd woman would have read something into the shock and agitation that Lark could see on her own face reflected in the bathroom mirror. Would have read something into her expression that really wasn't there, Lark assured herself. What did Lark care if Rand's old flame was returning in a few days? As she had assured Mrs. Quigley, *she* certainly wasn't falling for him.

Her expression was composed by the time she walked back into Mrs. Quigley's presence. Lark thanked her and returned the empty cup and cake dish.

"You listen to what I said, now," the older woman warned. "Don't go falling in love with Rand. You're only looking for trouble if you do."

Lark didn't mean to argue, but she couldn't help protesting. "Feelings change. All that was several years ago, wasn't it? Probably neither Rand nor Gloria feels as they once did."

"I wouldn't count on that," Mrs. Quigley said, her voice hard with warning. "Rand and Gloria are two of a kind, and what they want, they get, no matter who they have to run over or hurt or destroy in the process."

Lark paused in retying the protective bandanna around her hair. "What do you mean?" she asked slowly.

"There was talk that Rand made a lot of trips down to San Francisco." Mrs. Quigley nodded significantly.

"You mean he went to see Gloria while she was married?" Lark gasped in dismay.

"Rand isn't one to let a little thing like a marriage ceremony stand in the way of what he wants," Mrs. Quigley said, brows knit in disapproval. She paused and then added meaningfully, "And now Gloria has gotten a divorce."

Lark went back to work at a furious pace, vacuuming and scrubbing until her arms ached. But in spite of her busy physical activity, her mind kept straying back to Rand and all the things Mrs. Quigley had told her. She had already realized that Rand had a certain prowess where women were concerned, and, subconsciously, at least, realized she must be on guard against it. But she was surprised to find how dismaying she found the thought that Rand had carried on a relationship with Gloria while she was married, and probably had had something to do with the breakup of her marriage.

There was, it appeared, a great deal he had not told her, she thought unhappily.

But then she had to remind herself that he was under no obligation to tell her anything. He had aloofly informed her that she did not meet his requirements of sophistication and experience in a woman, and she certainly couldn't match Gloria Hammond's lush, dark beauty.

And yet, in spite of all that, some feminine instinct told her he was not entirely oblivious of her charms.

The following day, about midafternoon, Mrs. Quigley came up and practically insisted Lark take the remainder of the afternoon off. Mrs Quigley herself was driving into town to visit a niece.

It was a perfect spring day, unseasonably warm, and

Lark impulsively slipped into coral shorts and a sleeveless blouse that knotted at her slim waist. Her long legs looked unattractively pale to her own eyes, and she dabbed a bright polish on her toenails. She carried a blanket outside and lay in the sun for a while, but she found herself too restless to stay inactive for long.

She jumped up and wandered around, telling herself she hoped she did not run into Rand, but somehow disappointed when she discovered his pickup gone. She found a trail that led through heavy underbrush along the river to a low, rocky ledge overlooking a deep green pool below the roaring rapids. Then she spied a narrow dock reaching out into a calm area of backwater a little farther downstream. She had a sudden urge to dangle her bare feet in the water, something she hadn't done in years.

Quickly she made her way down to the dock and slipped her feet out of the sandals. The water was uncomfortably cold when she first tested it with a polish-tipped toe, but after a moment the cool effect was quite pleasant.

She lay back on the wooden dock, the slight motion from the moving water soothing and relaxing, and covered her eyes with her arm. The background roar of the river rapids was still there, but by now Lark was so accustomed to the sound that it was more soothing than disturbing. Everything was so peaceful that quite unintentionally she drifted off to sleep right there in the open sunlight.

When she opened her eyes, she was momentarily disoriented by the unfamiliar rocking motion beneath her body and the glare of sunlight in her eyes. Then a shadow fell across her face and she looked up, startled.

It was Rand, tall and powerful and somehow menacing as he loomed over her, hands on lean hips, dark eyes contemptuous.

"I must have fallen asleep," she said uneasily. "You startled me."

"I'm sure I did," he said harshly. "With Mrs. Quigley out of the way, I'm sure you thought you were all alone and could safely stop work and spend the afternoon loafing!"

Chapter Five

"That isn't true!" Lark gasped indignantly. "Mrs. Quigley gave me the remainder of the afternoon off before she went to visit her niece." She felt at a vulnerable disadvantage sprawled prone on the dock with Rand towering over her. His eyes swept over her bare midriff and rounded hips, down her slim legs to the frivolously painted toenails.

"That hardly sounds like her," Rand growled. "She usually complains that the girls who work at the lodge would rather flirt or loaf than work."

"If you don't believe me, you can ask Mrs. Quigley when she returns," Lark snapped. She scrambled to her feet and faced him defiantly. "I don't think I have to justify my every action to you. I would gamble that I've been working twice as hard as anyone else you might have chosen from among your 'inexhaustible supply of attractive young ladies'!"

"Mrs. Quigley has an exaggerated idea of the size of my circle of female friends," he commented dryly.

"I was under the impression she wasn't just referring to friends," Lark remarked tartly.

Rand had started away from her toward a boat on a trailer pulled by his pickup, parked a short distance away. He turned and gave her a long, calculating scowl but proceeded on toward the boat without further comment. Lark, balancing on one foot and then the other, managed to get her sandals on while keeping an eye on what he was doing.

He expertly backed the pickup and trailer down a narrow concrete ramp leading into the water. The trailer wheels were almost submerged before he stopped. Then, using a mechanical winch attached to the trailer, he let the boat down by cable until it floated free in the water. With a rope attached to the front end of the boat, he guided it to the dock and tied it securely. He seemed oblivious of Lark's presence now. He went back to the pickup and pulled the empty trailer to higher ground, leaving a trail of dripping water.

Lark inspected the boat before he returned to the dock. It was made of heavy aluminum but was completely different from the drift boats stacked in the storage building. This boat was wider and flatter, with seats for perhaps a dozen people toward the front. The driver evidently stood near the rear of the boat, where the steering apparatus was mounted on an upright column.

Rand jumped lithely from dock to boat and opened a rear engine compartment. He had removed his shirt, and the lean muscles in his powerful back rippled as he bent over the engine. He was not tan, and yet his skin lacked the winter paleness her own had. There was a certain raw virility about his naked torso that made some strange, unfamiliar feeling flicker through her own body. He glanced up, catching her scrutinizing him, and she felt herself flush again, afraid that strange, unfamiliar warmth within her might be all too obvious to him.

She walked along the edge of the dock, her gaze focused on the boat, and determinedly ignored the ruggedly muscled chest with its covering of fine dark masculine hair and the Levi's molded tautly to lean hips. She asked some questions about the boat, and he replied impersonally, telling her about the day trips the lodge offered on the area of the river where motorized craft were allowed. The jet boat, he indicated, had been at a shop in town for servicing and general checkup before the heavy-use season, and he was just putting it in the water for a trial run today.

He went back to working with something inside the engine compartment, and Lark, feeling herself dismissed, turned to leave.

"You'll forgive me for my remarks about your loafing behind Mrs. Quigley's back," he called after her, his voice more mocking than apologetic. "It's just that you seem to have this tendency to run away from unpleasant situations."

"I do not consider hard work an unpleasant situation," Lark shot back, blue eyes suddenly stormy.

Rand merely raised a dark, cynical eyebrow.

"And I don't think you are in any position to criticize, since you seem to have done some running away yourself!" she added, before thinking better of it.

"Just what do you mean by that?" he challenged.

Lark hesitated, immediately regretting that she had said anything, because it revealed that she and Mrs. Quigley had been discussing him. Her eyes evaded his, her fingers playing nervously with the knotted blouse.

"Well?" he prodded. "If you're going to make accusations, I think you should at least explain what you're talking about."

"I'm sure you know very well what I'm talking about!" she burst out, feeling cornered in spite of the open air and sunshine. "You did run away. Or at least walk out after some disagreement with your grandfather."

His eyes narrowed as he realized she now knew all about the large and powerful timber company and his past association with it. "And do you also know what the disagreement was about and who was right and who was wrong?"

"No, of course not," Lark faltered.

"Then I don't think you are in any position to make accusations or judgments," he snapped.

"But surely you could have worked out something," she protested. "Your leaving so abruptly must have left your grandfather and the company in a very awkward position."

"My grandfather is a stubborn, old-fashioned man who cannot or will not see that company management must change with the times. He is determined to teach me a lesson and show me that he and the company can get along fine without me." Rand stalked forward and untied the boat with a rough jerk, his face set and angry. His bared chest faced her, his raw maleness somehow challenging her.

"But you do intend to go back to the company some-day," Lark suggested.

"Perhaps."

"And perhaps it is *you* who are the stubborn one," she retorted, the words bursting out in spite of her knowledge that she was treading in deep, dangerous waters. "You're out to teach your grandfather a lesson by proving the company can't get along without you!"

He made no comment on the accusation, but his lips tightened warningly. "I'm going to take the boat for a run. Do you want to come along?" Neither his voice nor expression softened, and the words came out a challenge rather than an invitation.

Recklessly Lark responded with an angry challenge of her own. "Do you think you dare invite me? Won't Gloria object?"

"Well, I see you've been discussing not only my business life but my personal life as well." He jerked the knotted rope loose with an angry yank. "And neither is any of your concern!"

"You . . . you seemed to feel you had a right to accuse me of being unfair to Stanley," she faltered, uneasy under his uncompromising gaze.

"I don't think running out without talking to him face to face was fair," he said flatly.

"But it was fair for you to destroy Gloria's marriage!"

She quaked under the intensity of his harsh gaze, suddenly aware that he was not like the tame, accommodating men she had always known, that he could very well be provoked to physical violence. A muscle along his lean jawline jerked. Then he turned and flung the rope into the boat, following it with a surefooted leap that scorned a reply to her accusation.

A moment later the engine roared to life and the boat sped away from the dock, its speed increasing with astonishing rapidity. A jet of water ejected from the rear of the boat powerfully propelled the craft forward and seemed almost to lift it out of the water. Rand headed straight for the rapids, and Lark's heart pounded, thinking he surely couldn't make it through that boiling, surging white water. But the boat skimmed right over the rough water, seeming barely to touch it. Rand's hand never faltered on the throttle. A moment later boat and driver disappeared around the rocky bend in the river, though the roar and whine of the powerful engine echoed back at her.

Feeling shaken, Lark turned and headed back toward the lodge, her mind in turmoil. Obviously she had angered Rand almost to the exploding point with her reckless remarks. Remarks she probably had no right to make, she thought guiltily. His relationship with neither his grandfather nor Gloria was any of her affair, as he had caustically pointed out. But then, her relationship with Stanley was none of his affair, either, she thought defiantly.

It suddenly occurred to her that Rand's contemptuous attitude toward her "running away" from Stanley could be the result of his past relationship with Gloria Hammond. Had Rand been left with no more than a note of explanation when Gloria eloped with another man? And yet, even if that had happened, it evidently hadn't altered his basic feelings for her if he pursued her right into her marriage.

Lark did not tell Mrs. Quigley about the stormy encounter, and she saw Rand only at mealtimes, where he remained aloof and uncommunicative. Mrs. Quigley evidently sensed the tension between Lark and Rand, because she asked inquisitive questions, but Lark turned them aside with vague answers and concentrated on her work. A couple of days later the Hammonds arrived at the lodge in their luxurious motor home, having spent the winter in the sunny southwestern states and Mexico.

Lark fully expected to dislike them. Not, she assured herself, because they were the parents of the girl Rand had been, and perhaps still was, in love with. She simply doubted they could be particularly likable if they produced a daughter as willful and selfish as Gloria evidently was.

But, to her surprise, she did like them. Mr. Hammond was a stocky, balding man with a teasing sense of humor and cheerful blue eyes. Mrs. Hammond, who had a mature version of Gloria's beauty, was down-to-earth and friendly, complimentary about how sparkling clean the lodge and cabins looked.

Lark had mixed feelings when she realized Gloria was not with them. Lark's curiosity about the girl was intense, but deeper than the curiosity was an unexplained feeling of relief. The relief was short-lived, however, because she soon learned Gloria would be arriving in a few days, the delay caused by some complications in the property settlement of the divorce.

It was impossible for Lark to guess what Rand's feelings were about the delay. His expression, as usual, was inscrutable. But she noted that the Hammonds treated him with a sort of familiar affection. Unhappily she realized they probably already thought of him as their next son-in-law.

The routine of events around the lodge did not change appreciably with the Hammonds' return. They all ate together in the roomy kitchen, more like a congenial family than employer and employees. Lark's heavy scrubbing and cleaning tasks were about over, but there was a considerable amount of office work that needed to be done. Mrs. Hammond was delighted when she learned Lark could handle it. Lark's small fund of savings was growing, but it was still nowhere near enough to tide her over until she found a permanent job in San Diego.

And then, in a flurry of activity and excitement, Gloria Hammond arrived in a red Porsche overflowing with clothes and luggage. Lark watched the arrival from the window of the office, where she was answering mail inquiries about river trips. If Lark had hoped to find a few years had altered Gloria's beauty, she was disappointed. Her beauty was perhaps more contrived than that of the vibrant young girl in the trophy picture, but it was no less striking. She still had the cloud of dark hair, and her voluptuous figure was still slim-waisted.

With Gloria in the Porsche was another young woman, plain-faced but expensively dressed. Lark sourly suspected Gloria had brought the girl along solely as a foil for her own lush beauty. Three more attractive young couples arrived in separate cars. The entire group was bright and noisy, with a general air of being accustomed to good times and an abundance of money.

Lark missed seeing the actual initial encounter between Gloria and Rand, but she heard Gloria call his name and saw her run toward the boat-storage building. Lark's imagination filled in the rest.

From that moment on, everything changed. The relaxed, easygoing atmosphere of the lodge quickened. Meals, except for the help, moved to the dining room, where the mealtime conversation was bright and animated. Rand obviously had a status superior to that of mere employee, however, and ate with the family and guests. Lark dreaded the idea that she might have to wait on table, but Mrs. Hammond called one of the girls employed by the lodge the previous summer, and the girl started work immediately

The girl, Pam Memovich, moved into the girls' dorm with Lark. She was a bit on the messy side, but good-natured and fun. She cheerfully admitted she'd had a wild crush on Rand since last summer and, in her somewhat exaggerated, breathless style, thought him simply "fabulous" and "fantastic." She had not met Gloria previously but quickly took an aversion to her and delighted in doing wickedly amusing imitations of Gloria's hip-swinging walk and seductive sideways glances.

Gloria herself took little more notice of the lodge help than she did of the furniture. She and her friends slept late every morning, but there was a continual flurry of activity once they were up. Rides in the jet boat, tennis, outdoor barbecues. Rand was always included in the activities. Gloria acted both flirtatious and possessive toward him. Rand did not appear to encourage Gloria, so far as Lark could tell. But neither, she noted unhappily, was he exactly fighting Gloria off.

The first white-water river trip for paying guests was not scheduled until the following week, but Gloria and her friends decided they wanted a private camping trip down the river.

In spite of her aversion to Gloria, Lark was interested in the preparations for the trip. Three rafts would be going, two to carry passengers, one loaded with supplies and equipment. Rand, as head guide, would supervise everything and handle one raft. Two younger guides, experienced as helpers from the previous year, would handle the other rafts. The supplies were carefully packed in big waterproof boxes, each meal planned ahead of time and everything necessary for its preparation grouped together. Perishable items went in insulated chests along with ice. Lark was particularly intrigued by the preparation of eggs for the trip. Each was carefully cracked open and, without breaking the yolk, slipped into a plastic jar until the container looked as if it were full of yellow eyes. Mrs. Quigley assured her that packed this way the eggs could take a great deal of jouncing and bouncing through the river rapids. Cooked ham and roast beef went along for lunches, but the guides would cook steaks and chicken for dinners.

Lark went down to the small dock to see the supplies loaded and securely lashed on the raft and then waited in the background to watch the high-spirited group depart. If Rand noticed her, he gave no sign of it. He was busy making sure the weight was properly distributed on the supply raft. Gloria, without exactly hanging on to him, conveyed a proprietary attitude that brooked no interference. She was not, Lark observed caustically, exactly a brokenhearted divorcée.

Finally passengers and gear were loaded, and Rand gave a signal to shove off. Lark watched until the yellow-and-black rafts bobbed out of sight around a bend in the river, wishing she were going along. Feeling vaguely dispirited, she made her way back to the lodge and tackled the latest batch of correspondence and reservations. The lodge seemed empty and too quiet with the noisy, vivacious group gone, though Lark was uncomfortably aware the feeling of emptiness came more from Rand's absence than anything else.

She paused in her office work, her pert chin resting on one hand as she gazed broodingly out the window. Was it possible, she wondered unhappily, that she was doing exactly what Mrs. Quigley had warned against, falling in love with Rand? No, that couldn't be, she assured herself. Love made you feel joyous and alive, happy and wonderful, and that certainly wasn't what she felt, especially not when she knew Rand would be in Gloria's constant company for the next three days. And nights. And yet, if she wasn't falling in love with him, why should that matter so much to her? Why should his aloof coldness ever since their stormy scene at the boat dock make her feel so unhappy and dispirited?

Sometime during the day, Lark noted a few clouds drifting in and occasionally blotting out the spring sunshine. By evening the sky was overcast, and the following afternoon a steady rain started. Lark worried about how Rand was coping in the weather and wondered if it made the river even more dangerous, but Mrs. Quigley and Pam were less generous in their thoughts. Mrs. Quigley openly hoped Gloria got sick and tired of Oregon rain and scurried back to California. Pam did a wickedly amusing parody of Gloria trying to keep thrusting breasts and rounded derriere dry in a rainstorm.

The schedule called for the group to arrive at Foster Bar, the takeout point on the river, on the afternoon of the fourth day. Mr. Hammond was going to drive the pickup and pull the trailer on which to haul the rafts back. Mrs. Hammond planned to drive the station wagon down to provide transportation for Gloria and her guests.

But on the third day, Lark answered the office phone and heard one of the younger guides, wet and disgruntled, say they had speeded up the trip because of the weather. He had hiked in the rain to a nearby lodge to call, and would someone, he requested plaintively, please come and get them *now?*

That presented a new problem. Mrs. Hammond had taken the station wagon on a shopping trip to the neighboring small city of Medford and wasn't expected home until evening. That meant someone would have to drive the big van the lodge ordinarily used to transport larger groups of guests. Mr. Hammond looked inquiringly at Lark. Finally, after a moment's hesitation, she nodded. She had not driven the lodge's van before, but her father had once owned a similar van and she had driven it.

They departed a scarce twenty minutes later, Mr. Hammond leading the way in the pickup. Shortly after they left the lodge, he turned away from the river, taking a winding road up through the mountains. In the driving rain Lark was uncertain whether or not this was the same road from which she had taken that fateful turn onto Robertson Timber Company property. Mr. Hammond did not drive fast, but he was often out of sight around a bend, and Lark felt isolated and alone in the wildly beautiful mountains. The only traffic she encountered was a few loaded log trucks. Her heart leaped to her throat whenever she met one of the big trucks on the narrow road. There hardly seemed room to pass, but somehow she always squeezed by.

At some point they reached the top of the grade through the mountains and started down the other side. There were still patches of snow in places along the road. Eventually they wound back down to the river and crossed a bridge over the surly-looking Rogue and finally reached Foster Bar. It was merely a rocky, brushy area with a boat ramp leading into the water. Right now the ramp was deserted except for the wet group huddled under an overturned raft braced at an angle for shelter. Lark donned a slicker and rain hat before stepping out into the pouring rain. Mr. Hammond turned the pickup around in order to back the trailer toward the beached rafts.

If Lark thought Gloria would be grateful for the quick response to the party's call for help, she was wrong. Gloria strode forward, the dark hair that usually drifted to her shoulders in a sensuous cloud now plastered wetly to her head. Devoid of makeup, her face looked older and harsher.

"It took you long enough to get here," Gloria snapped. "We're soaked and freezing." She didn't wait for a comment. She motioned her wet companions toward the van.

Rand strode toward Lark, the momentary look of surprise on his face quickly replaced by disapproval. "What are you doing here?" he demanded.

He was dressed in Levi's and denim jacket, hatless, obviously wet from head to foot, and yet paying no heed to his uncomfortable situation. Water dripped from his crisp hair to the wet collar of the jacket. Somehow the pouring rain and his utter disdain of it only emphasized his powerful masculinity, a raw maleness that was as much a part of him as his dark good looks and broad shoulders.

"Well?" he prompted curtly.

Briefly Lark explained about Mrs. Hammond's absence and how she herself happened to be here.

"I don't think you ought to be driving these roads in this kind of weather with no more experience than you've had," he snapped.

"You wouldn't want Gloria and her friends left out in the rain until her mother returned, would you?" Lark retorted angrily. She had actually worried about him out on the river in this storm, and all he had to say was that he thought her too incompetent to drive his precious Gloria through the mountains!

Rand opened his mouth to say something else, no doubt some even more contemptuous remark, Lark thought furiously, but Gloria's imperious call from the van interrupted.

"Lark, please don't stand around talking all day. We want to go home *now*." Before Gloria rolled up the window, Lark caught a few words of her irritated comment to her friends inside, something about the poor quality of help available these days.

"If you'll excuse me, it appears I'm wanted," Lark said icily.

A muscle in Rand's jaw tightened. "Be careful. These roads can be more dangerous than you realize."

For a moment she thought she saw concern in his expression, but then she remembered it was only concern for Gloria, of course. "You may be sure I'll take good care of your precious Gloria," she flung over her shoulder as she headed for the van.

He made no comment, but Lark realized he might not even have heard her sarcastic remark in the rising wind. When she glanced back again, he was already helping lift one of the rafts onto the trailer.

Lark started the engine of the van to get the heater going and dug out the vacuum bottles of hot coffee that Mrs. Quigley had sent along. As they headed toward home, the ill humor of the group seemed to lift. The guests started removing damp clothing, and the windows steamed over.

One of the young wives finally laughed as she ran her fingers through wet, tangled hair. "I feel like a drowned rat."

The other wife wrinkled her nose. "And we smell even worse. But this coffee is a lifesaver."

"Speaking of lifesaving, wasn't that something the way Rand swam out and hauled that guy in?" one of the men remarked.

Lark didn't mean to say anything. She was all too aware of her subservient position as driver, but the shocked words were out before she could stop them. "Rand swam in the river in this weather? What happened?"

One of the women went on to explain that just after they made camp the previous evening a drift boat had overturned in rapids just above the campsite. The two occupants had foolishly not been wearing life jackets. One man made it to shore, but the other was being swept downstream when Rand plunged in and rescued him.

"He was magnificent," she said with an appreciative roll of her eyes. She glanced sideways at her husband, smiling teasingly. "If I weren't already married . . ."

"Hands off Rand. He's spoken for," Gloria said. She laughed and her voice was light, but there was a definite undertone of warning.

Though the retelling of the story had been in response to Lark's startled question, Lark knew she was already forgotten as the chatter became livelier. There was talk about Rainie Falls and Wildcat Rapids, Mule Creek Canyon and Blossom Bar. Soon the more uncomfortable aspects of the adventure had taken on a humorous aspect as they talked about wet feet and damp sleeping bags and a bear that wandered into camp and raided an ice chest before the two young guides chased him off.

"By the way, just where were you and Rand during the bear episode?" one of the young women inquired a trifle coyly.

Gloria tilted her head. "Oh, we were taking a walk and . . . ummm . . . enjoying the scenery." She said it in such a way that left no doubt but that they were doing something other than enjoying the scenery, and everyone laughed.

Lark just kept her eyes on the road, thankful that she didn't have to pretend amusement.

Nearing the highest point of elevation on the return trip, the rain actually turned to a spitting snow for a time. Lark was glad when the road started downhill again, suddenly aware as the wheels skidded slightly that she was indeed carrying a heavy load of responsibility. The noisy group inside the van didn't seem to notice weather or road, however, and Lark was beginning to suspect one of the men had spiked the coffee with something alcoholic.

Finally they were past what Lark thought was the worst of the winding road and she was just beginning to relax a little. Then the van rounded a curve to a scene of utter chaos.

A log truck lay on its side, the cab in a ditch and the trailer angled crazily across the road. Logs were scattered across the roadway like giant toothpicks. The accident had evidently just happened, because some of the logs were still moving, rolling and careening into each other, smashing over and through rocks and brush and trees along the road.

Lark took it all in in one stunned instant punctuated by a sudden scream of terror from one of the women behind her. Lark's own throat was too frozen to scream.

The road was blocked. There was no way through that tangled barrier of overturned truck and rolling logs. She slammed on the brakes, but the tires skidded head-long toward the downed truck.

There was no time to weigh the pros and cons of any course of action. Some basic instinct for survival simply flashed the message that there was only one way out, and Lark took it.

She battled with the steering wheel for control, feeling the van buck and twist like a live thing beneath her, and then it hurtled up the steep embankment only inches from the downed truck cab.

For a second the van hung there against the steep dirt bank, and then slowly it slipped backward and came to rest at an angle above the truck. Lark was only dimly aware of a whirl of voices and shouts around her. She leaned her head against her arms on the steering wheel, her mind numb and stunned.

Then the door beside her opened a few inches. The dirt bank prevented any further opening.

"Hey, lady, you okay?" a concerned male voice asked. Numbly Lark realized he must be the log-truck driver, unhurt in spite of his spectacular accident. "That was some quick thinking. I didn't think there was any way you could avoid one hell of a crash!"

Behind Lark, Gloria and her friends were a confused tangle of arms and legs and wet clothing and spilled coffee. It was impossible to get out the front doors of the van, but finally everyone piled out the rear luggage doors. By that time the burly log-truck driver had set out warning flares on either side of the blocked road-way.

Everyone was dazed and shaken. Even Gloria seemed momentarily subdued. There appeared to be no serious injuries, but the quiet, plain-faced girl had bumped her nose and was bleeding profusely. Lark looked around frantically for something to help stanch the flow. Finally she jerked off her own sweater and held it to the girl's nose.

Lark stood there with the girl, patting her shoulder reassuringly. She doubted the bleeding was serious, but she knew a nosebleed could be frightening, and the amount of blood was certainly terrifying. Over the girl's shoulder Lark could see the perilous path the van had taken, the dark skid marks on the road and the ruts left by the tires as the vehicle hurtled up the dirt embankment. Only a split second's delay in turning the wheel and the van would have crashed headlong into the sprawled truck.

Finally the girl's nosebleed slowed and she dug in her own pocket for a supply of tissues. "Don't mind me," she said, sounding embarrassed. "I get these if I so much as stub my toe. They aren't as terrible as they look. And I'll replace your sweater."

"Don't worry about it. It wasn't much more than an old rag anyway," Lark said comfortingly. However, rag or not, the sweater had been keeping her warm, and now she realized she was shivering in the damp cold.

She was looking at the sweater in dismay when she heard the squeal of brakes around the corner in response to the warning flares the truck driver had set out. A moment later the lodge pickup nosed cautiously around the curve, Rand at the wheel.

The pickup had hardly stopped before Rand was out of it and racing toward the strangely subdued group huddled at the edge of the roadway. Gloria stepped out of the group, but Rand brushed on by her, his eyes locked on Lark's bloodstained sweater.

"My God," he said, "what happened?"

Lark thought she was in complete control of herself. After all, the danger was over now, neither she nor anyone else badly injured. But suddenly the world reeled dizzily around her, and in a kind of horrified astonishment she felt her knees buckle beneath her just as Rand reached her.

Chapter Six

Lark didn't lose consciousness. She simply could not seem to make her rubbery knees work properly to hold her upright. She felt foolish and embarrassingly exposed stretched out on the damp roadside with everyone peering down at her curiously. She struggled to sit up, but Rand's hand firmly held her down.

The rain had stopped, but air and ground were still damp and chill. Lark shivered, and Rand immediately jerked his jacket off and covered her with it, tucking the edges under her body. The jacket was still slightly damp, but it held the warmth of Rand's body, a warmth that penetrated and soothed her chilled flesh.

"I'm all right." Her voice came out a hoarse croak. "Really I am. The blood was from Miss Richter's nosebleed. I'm fine."

In spite of Lark's protests, Rand gave her a quick checkup for broken bones, saying that in cases of shock people sometimes didn't realize how badly they were injured or even that they were injured at all. His hands on her body felt strong and capable, and in spite of the awkward situation, Lark felt a quiver of sensual reaction to his touch. She held herself tensely rigid to avoid revealing anything of her internal agitation to him.

Finally, bracing her with his arm, Rand helped her to

her feet. "I can't find anything wrong. You're sure you feel all right?"

"Yes, I'm fine now."

"You're sure? When I think what could have happened . . ." His arm tightened protectively around her shoulders.

The touch and the worried concern in Rand's eyes made Lark's pulse race, and her knees felt rubbery again, though for a different reason this time. He helped her to the pickup and told her in tones that left no room for argument that she was to stay there and keep warm. He leaned toward her, and for one heart-stopping moment Lark thought he was going to kiss her, but he just squeezed her hand and told her not to worry. Gratefully, Lark also realized that not once had Rand made any "I-told-you-so" remark about the dangers of driving this road, that his voice and actions showed only concern. A concern, she thought with a sense of wonderment, that he had not shown for Gloria.

After making sure Lark was warm and safe in the pickup, Rand efficiently set about taking care of the other problems. Using long-handled hooked tools from the log truck, Rand and the truck driver started prying the logs out of the roadway. While Rand was working on the logs, Mr. Hammond came to check on Lark. His cheerful but piercing blue eyes looked her over.

"You're not hurt? You look rather pale."

"I'm fine," Lark insisted, for at least the third time that afternoon.

"You certainly used your head," Mr. Hammond complimented. "Everyone has been telling me how quickly you responded to the crisis."

"I'm afraid I can't even remember doing anything," Lark admitted honestly.

"This probably isn't an appropriate time to mention this, while you're still upset about the accident, but I'll bring it up so you can be thinking about it. Mrs. Hammond has been very pleased with your work in the office, and I must say I'm extremely impressed with what you did here today in averting a real tragedy. I'd like to offer you a job for the full summer season, if you're interested."

Lark was so surprised that she was momentarily at a loss for words. Mr. Hammond misinterpreted the delay, taking astonishment for reluctance.

"Your salary would be larger, of course. You'd be driving this road twice a week, plus doing the office work, and that involves a lot of responsibility. We'd expect you to stay the full season, however, if you accepted."

Glancing out the mud-specked window, Lark wondered if Gloria knew what her father was doing. She suspected not. She further suspected Gloria would not be at all pleased if she did know. And what about Rand? Lark's heart did an unexpected flip-flop. Would he want her to stay?

Lark finally murmured noncommittally that she would think about the offer, but Mr. Hammond's appreciative comments and compliments left her with a warm glow. And frightening as the accident had been, the knowledge that she had reacted swiftly to a crisis gave her a good feeling of satisfaction and self-confidence.

By that time, Rand and the truck driver had managed to clear a narrow, car-width space between the logs. Next Rand unhooked the boat trailer from the pickup and used the pickup to pull the van free. It was all done smoothly and efficiently, without waste motion. Rand insisted Lark ride in the pickup back to the lodge. Benny, one of the younger guides, drove the van. Lark caught sight of Gloria frowning at her from the van, obviously not at all pleased with this turn of events.

That night Lark thought for a long time about whether or not to accept Mr. Hammond's offer. One part of her warned, almost screamed: *Go.* Go now, before you fall in love with Rand and wind up with a broken heart. Her reaction to Rand's protective concern

today was warning enough that her heart was much too
vulnerable for safety.

But another part of her coaxed: *Stay*. Stay . . . why?
Because she wanted to be near him. Arrogant and infuriating as he often could be, he had also been tender and
gentle today. Her heart suddenly beat faster at the
memory of his arms holding her as her knees buckled
beneath her, and the intimate feel of his sinewy thigh
pressed against hers on the drive home.

The next morning she sought out Mr. Hammond and
accepted his offer, rationalizing, in the broad light of
day, that she really had no choice, since she hadn't yet
saved enough money to tide her over in San Diego.

Gloria's guests departed later that day in the same
flurry of excitement with which they had arrived. Only
the plain-faced young woman came to say good-bye to
Lark, telling her again how magnificently she had
reacted at the accident. The compliment left Lark with a
nice warm feeling, a feeling that cooled swiftly as she
looked up from her office desk only minutes later and
saw Gloria standing at the counter regarding her appraisingly.

"Was there something you wanted?" Lark asked
uneasily.

"No, not exactly. Actually, I'm more interested in
what *you* want," Gloria answered. She gave her dark
hair a toss and came around the counter to perch on the
corner of Lark's desk. She wore a musky perfume that
would have been overpowering on some women but
somehow seemed to fit her lush beauty.

Lark felt confused by this ambiguous approach. "I'm
sorry," she murmured. "I don't understand what you're
talking about."

"Rand, of course," Gloria said candidly. "I understand
you've decided to stay on here, and it's written all over
your face whenever you look at him that you're falling
in love with him."

"That isn't true!" Lark denied. But at the very moment the words were spoken, she knew that it *was* true. Last night she had toyed with the dangerous possibility that she might fall in love with Rand, but she had been deceiving herself. It was too late to say she was merely "falling in love" with Rand. It had taken only those few moments of tenderness from him after the accident to send her over the precipice, fling her headlong into the giddy whirlpool of love. Lark felt her skin burn as she realized her face had all along revealed what she had not earlier acknowledged even to herself, what it was no doubt revealing at this very moment. That she was in love with him, heart and body and soul.

Gloria lifted a dark eyebrow. "You see?" she said, as if Lark's jumbled thought processes were an open book to her.

"I . . . I really don't know why you're talking to me about this," Lark said, struggling for composure. She rattled and shuffled some papers on the desk to make a show of being busy. "I have a great deal of work to do."

"It can wait," Gloria said arrogantly.

Lark lifted her eyes. She would not admit aloud that what Gloria said about her feelings for Rand was true, but she knew any denial would ring hollow. "I can't see that my personal feelings are any concern of yours," she finally said stiffly.

Gloria shrugged. "Perhaps not. But since I happen to be in love with Rand myself, I intend to make it my concern." She stood up suddenly and moved around, studying Lark. "You're very attractive, of course. Not Rand's usual type, but quite attractive in a naive, vulnerable sort of way."

The jibe, so similar to Rand's own assessment, burned into Lark, but she managed to keep her voice calm when she said, "Perhaps he has changed 'types,' then."

Unexpectedly, Gloria laughed, a cynical, humorless sound. She reached into a compartment under the counter, brought out a package of filter-tip cigarettes, and lit one. "Don't deceive yourself. Rand is just out to teach me a lesson."

Lark didn't want to continue this conversation and desperately searched for the strength to tell Gloria she was not interested in hearing any details of her relationship with Rand. Instead she found herself saying with a dry throat, "What do you mean?"

"How long have you known Rand?" Gloria asked abruptly, eyeing Lark appraisingly. She answered the question herself without waiting for Lark to reply. "A few weeks. I've known him most of my life." She inhaled on the cigarette, exhaled, and studied the blue smoke as it rose above her dark hair. "A few years ago I made a disastrous mistake. I thought I was tired of the quiet life here. I thought I wanted a city life, city excitement. A city man. I eloped and married David Riegal and went to live in San Francisco."

In spite of herself, Lark found a certain fascination in listening to Gloria's tale. "And you weren't . . . happy?" she faltered.

"I was miserable," Gloria said flatly. "I knew within a few months that I should have stayed here and married Rand."

"And so you kept up a relationship with Rand while you were married?" Lark dared to ask, somehow hoping Mrs. Quigley's suspicions were wrong.

The hope died as Gloria stubbed out the cigarette, her eyes narrowing. "I don't believe I care to discuss that."

"No," Lark agreed faintly. "I suppose not."

"In any case, as you no doubt know, I'm divorced now," Gloria went on.

"Yes," Lark echoed. "You're divorced now. But there's nothing definite between you and Rand." She broke off awkwardly, embarrassed to hear the humiliating hope in her own voice.

"No," Gloria agreed, "there's nothing definite." Surprisingly, she sounded more resigned than worried or angry. She inspected her long fingernails and sighed. "I told you. Rand is teaching me a lesson."

"I don't understand."

"It's really very simple. Rand was furious when I married David." Gloria laughed lightly. "And, as I'm sure you've already learned, Rand is not one to get over his anger easily."

Lark could not argue that point. She could imagine Rand's dark fury at losing the woman he loved. A loss, Lark thought hollowly, he had refused to accept without a battle. And now he had won, because Gloria was free again.

Gloria sighed again. "Men are so silly, aren't they, with their foolish pride and stubbornness? But I know I must simply be patient until Rand feels I have learned my lesson for daring to defy him."

The words suddenly sounded jarringly familiar to Lark. This was exactly what she had suspected Rand of doing to his grandfather, stubbornly walking out until the old man acknowledged he had learned his lesson, that he was wrong and Rand was right.

"I'm only telling you all this for your own good," Gloria went on self-righteously. "I wouldn't want to see you hurt."

"I think I can take care of myself," Lark finally said curtly. She jammed a piece of paper into the typewriter to end the conversation.

"Don't say I didn't warn you," Gloria said. "Rand isn't above using someone else in his plan to teach me a lesson and show me that two can play the same game."

Lark typed furiously, sending the keys flying across the page, slamming the return carriage back time and again. When she finally paused and looked up, Gloria was gone, leaving only the lingering scent of her heady perfume. Ruefully Lark realized nothing of what she had typed made sense. Slowly she crumpled the paper and tossed it at the wastebasket.

She didn't want to believe any part of what Gloria

had said. She surely did *not* believe that Gloria had any concern over whether or not Lark might get hurt. Gloria had hardly realized Lark was alive until Rand showed some interest in her. But what Gloria had said about Rand's stubborn determination to teach her a lesson before taking her back was all too plausible. Mrs. Quigley, too, had warned Lark against falling in love with Rand, warned that Rand would not care whom he might hurt or destroy in order to get what he wanted. And if what Rand wanted was to teach Gloria a lesson before taking her back, Lark had no doubt but that he would ruthlessly use her to aid in that scheme.

No, that wasn't true! Lark denied almost frantically to herself. Rand had been honestly concerned and worried about her at the scene of the accident. He hadn't pretended all that merely for Gloria's benefit—had he?

A few days later the paying guests started arriving for the first white-water trip of the season. By that time Lark had passed the necessary chauffeur's driving test and was legally qualified to transport guests from the end of the river trips back to the lodge. She had avoided Rand those last few days. Or perhaps, she thought unhappily, Rand had been avoiding her, since he seemed to have plenty of time for swimming or tennis with Gloria.

Lark was tempted to seek him out and bluntly ask if there was any truth to Gloria's claim, sure he would furiously deny everything. But another part of her was afraid to ask. Afraid of his fury for daring to snoop in his affairs, perhaps even more afraid he would admit it was all true, that he was in love with Gloria and temporarily punishing her for her audacity or foolishness in running off with another man.

Now that Lark had taken over the office duties, she normally didn't help serve meals to the guests, but on the evening before the first white-water river trip, she was pressed into service to help with the outdoor barbecue. While she set the patio tables with colorful pottery plates and cups, she caught snatches of Rand talking to the guests on the deck above. He was telling them what they could expect on the river, how to handle themselves in case of emergency, how to pack their gear for the trip. He mentioned the bear raid of the last trip, drawing excited squeals from some of the women. He showed them what the annoying rash-and-itch-producing poison-oak shrub looked like and also suggested they keep a sharp eye out for rattlesnakes around camp. Afterward everyone streamed out to the barbecue grill, where Mrs. Quigley was broiling steaks.

Lark, Pam, and Mrs. Quigley ate in the kitchen after the guests were served. Later, when Lark was gathering up soiled dishes from the patio tables, she heard an unfamiliar voice at her side.

"Now, what is a lovely, delicate little thing like you doing carrying that big stack of plates around?" the man asked disapprovingly.

Lark glanced up, mentally connecting the florid, middle-aged face with the name "Mr. Desmond" on the lodge reservations list. He was carrying a glass that was almost empty except for the clinking ice cubes. Lark recalled that he had paid in advance for river trips for six of the other guests. A businessman entertaining clients, she assumed.

Mr. Desmond was waiting for an answer, and finally Lark said lightly, "It's just part of my job."

"What's there to do for fun around this place, anyway?" the man complained. "No nightclubs, no dancing, no entertainment."

It was on the tip of Lark's tongue to say tartly that if he wanted nightclubs and entertainment he should have taken his clients to Las Vegas, but that was hardly the thing a courteous employee said to a guest. She moved to one side, trying to get around Mr. Desmond's bulky figure, but he sidestepped, blocking her way. Lark glanced around and saw Rand watching her, an odd expression on his face. Gloria was looking at her too.

"Here, let me have these," the man said, unexpectedly reaching for the stack of dishes. "I'll carry them in for you, and maybe we can get to know each other better."

Short of grabbing the dishes back and making an awkward scene, Lark didn't know what she could do about the situation. She was aware of disapproving eyes following as she and Mr. Desmond made their way up to the kitchen.

Lark thought she could make some excuse to stay in the kitchen and end the uncomfortable situation, but Mr. Desmond gaily informed Mrs. Quigley that he was stealing Lark for a walk along the river.

Lark was at a loss as to what to do now. She didn't want to be rude to a paying guest, but she didn't care to go walking with him either. Finally she said brightly, "Why don't we find your friends and we'll all walk down and look at the rafts you'll be using tomorrow."

To Lark's dismay, they found that the after-dinner group had already dispersed, and Mr. Desmond's clients were nowhere to be seen. Mr. Desmond clutched Lark's hand. Uneasily she tried to pull her fingers away, but his damp grip only tightened.

"Please, Mr. Desmond . . ."

"Call me Syd."

"I really should be helping in the kitchen. I don't want to lose my job."

"You won't lose your job," Mr. Desmond assured her. "With all the money I'm spending here, I think I have a little influence."

He smiled at her, a smile that in the dusky light looked more like a leer. By now he had pulled her into the shadows of the trees along the trail to the river, and his other hand slid around her slim waist. Lark gasped in surprise and then suddenly she was furious. This man whom she didn't even know, who had hardly spoken a word to her until a bare ten or fifteen minutes ago, obviously seemed to think he had the right to run his hands all over her just because he was a free-spending customer and she a captive employee. A moment later his lips actually sought hers, his hot breath repulsive.

The suddenness of the unpleasant situation and the man's utter gall and crudeness sickened Lark. A full moon was just rising over the mountains, and over Mr. Desmond's shoulder Lark could see several people strolling around enjoying the pleasant, moonlit evening. A scream would bring someone running—perhaps even Rand! But the thought of anyone seeing her here, mauled by this repugnant man, was suddenly more than she could bear. His hands were moving boldly over her, but with a sudden clarity she saw him for what he was. A bully. And bullies were basically cowards.

"Mr. Desmond, if you do not take your hands off me this minute, I am going to scream my head off," Lark said suddenly, keeping her voice flatly cold and emotionless. "And then I will file legal charges against you."

The man lifted his head, his manner suddenly wary. "You wouldn't dare," he said thickly.

"Just try me and you'll find out," Lark challenged. She honestly didn't know if she was bluffing or not, but Mr. Desmond evidently decided not to take the risk.

"I was just trying to have a little fun," he whined, sounding injured. "Just trying to show you a good time." He took a step backward and wiped his forehead with a handkerchief.

A little fun! A good time! Lark was so angry and upset she was shaking, and she had half a mind to scream and let develop what might. Suddenly she couldn't bear to be in Mr. Desmond's repulsive presence a moment longer, and she turned and fled down the trail along the river.

Tears streamed down her face as she ran. She didn't know why. It was all over now. But, as with the accident on the road, there seemed to be some sort of delayed reaction that set in after she had managed a crisis satisfactorily. She ran until the trail ended at a rocky point below the dock and slumped gasping to the ground. She felt soiled, dirty, with the touch of the man's hands still on her. There was a sense of unreality in Lark's mind about what had just happened, a feeling of incredulousness that it had happened at all. It was all so abrupt, so unexpected. The nerve of the man, she thought, anger boiling again. The utter gall!

A shadow fell across Lark, blotting out the moonlight. For a moment she almost panicked, thinking it was Mr. Desmond who had followed her.

Then she recognized the tall, commanding figure. "Oh, Rand. It's you," she murmured, relieved that it was not Mr. Desmond and yet not eager to encounter Rand just now either. At the moment, all she wanted was to be alone until the feeling of revulsion wore off.

"I saw you race down here as if you were running for your life. What happened?" Rand asked sharply.

"Nothing," Lark murmured evasively.

"*Nothing*? I can hardly believe that!" he snapped, looking down at her suspiciously. "I saw Desmond talking to you earlier. What did he want?"

Lark swallowed convulsively. "He said he wanted to . . . to get better acquainted."

"By dragging you under a tree and pawing you?"

Lark's breath caught at the complete accuracy of Rand's statement. When she didn't reply, he prodded angrily. "Isn't that what happened?"

"Yes, yes, it is!" She shuddered, covering her face with her hands, trying to blot it all out. "It was all so awful, so ugly . . ."

"And you just stood there and let him paw you?" Rand asked angrily. "You must have known I was nearby. Why didn't you scream? Why did you let him get away with it?"

Lark uncovered her face, shocked by the intimation that she had somehow done something wrong. "I didn't just let him get away with it," she said defensively.

She rose to her feet, brushing dirt and bits of dead grass from her clothing. Rand's back was to the moonlight, his face in shadows, so she could not see his expression. But she did not need to see it to know the anger written there.

"Didn't you?" he flared. "I can tell you exactly what you did. You ran away. It seems to be what you do best."

"That isn't fair!" Lark gasped. "I didn't want to upset everyone with an unpleasant scene and—"

"Of course not," he said contemptuously. "You'd rather run away from an unpleasant scene."

Lark drew herself up to her full height to face his formidable figure defiantly. Suddenly her own anger, targeted only on the repulsive Mr. Desmond, enlarged to include Rand. "And sometimes there are better ways to handle an ugly scene than with physical violence," she said, her voice icy in spite of a certain tremulousness.

"Such as?" His voice was deadly skeptical.

"A threat to scream stopped Mr. Desmond as effectively as a scream itself. And I warned him that if I did find it necessary to scream, I wouldn't stop there. I would file charges against him. And I do not care for your attitude that I was somehow partly to blame!"

Rand was between the rocky point on which Lark stood and the trail back to the lodge, and she angrily stepped around him. A hard-muscled arm shot out and stopped her. As he turned, moonlight sculptured angular shadows across his face.

"I didn't mean to imply that you were to blame." His expression was still harshly uncompromising and his voice held no apology, but he seemed to relent slightly in his arrogant contempt. His firm grip on her arm tightened still further. "It's just that I hate to think of him touching you like that."

Lark's heart suddenly began to pound erratically at the implication in his words, and her lips parted as she looked up at him uncertainly. He was looking down at her in a possessive way that she found strangely intoxicating.

"I . . . I'm trying to make you understand that I didn't put up with it," she said tremulously. "I just handled it in the way that seemed best at the moment. And then I ran because I couldn't stand to be around him another moment."

"Perhaps you did handle it in the best way, then," he acknowledged. His voice hardened as he added, "Mr. Desmond can be thankful that you chose to handle it the way you did."

He flexed his hands, and there was no mistaking the threat in his voice. Lark shivered lightly.

"You're still upset," he observed suddenly.

"No—"

Her objections were muffled against his chest as he pulled her to him, his arms strong and secure around her. For a moment she resisted, and then she melted against him, taking refuge in his comforting embrace, sheltered from the ugliness of the earlier encounter. They just stood there for a long minute, and she could feel the powerful beat of his heart, reassuring in its strength, and the protective security of his encircling arms. Finally he lifted one hand to tilt her chin up to face him.

"Feeling better?" he asked. His face in the silvery moonlight had a sculptured look, a night god come to life.

She couldn't speak. She could only nod. He dipped his head, his lips brushing hers lightly for a moment, as if in consolation for the ugly moments she had suffered.

Lark held herself rigid, determinedly forcing back the wild reaction that surged through her, a reaction that was totally inappropriate to the lightness and brevity of the kiss. One part of her wanted to turn and flee again, away from him and this strange reaction within her, but her feet were riveted to the rocky earth. Somewhere in the background of her mind she heard the endless roar of the river. Or was it her own blood pounding in her ears?

"You're shaking," he murmured, lips against her temple.

Lark's eyes flew open, and she realized in dismay that in spite of her rigid determination to reveal nothing of the tumult within her, she was trembling. She looked into the hollowed shadows of his eyes and saw a dark gleam that told her he was fully aware of his impact on her.

"I . . . I'm just a little cold," Lark murmured defensively.

His arms tightened around her, drawing her closer against the hard, warm length of his body. One hand massaged the small of her back, sending fiery shivers up her spine and fanning an unfamiliar smoldering heat deep within her. His lips feathered tantalizing kisses on her temple. She felt the sinewy muscles of his chest against her breasts.

"Are you warmer now?" His warm lips and breath murmured against her ear, and she was aware of sensitive nerve endings she had never realized she possessed until they now awakened under his touch.

"Don't . . ." she protested helplessly.

"Don't what?" His teasing lips played with her earlobe. "You said you were chilly, and I'm just trying to keep you warm."

She felt rather than heard the silent laughter vibrating within him, and suddenly Lark was furious. He was playing with her, laughing at her because she was naive and inexperienced, amusing himself with the power he had to make her tremble with strange, unfamiliar desires.

"I'm going back to the lodge," she announced thickly. She put the palms of her hands on his chest and pushed, but she might as well have struggled against a stone wall.

He leaned his head back to look down at her, without releasing the hold on her hips that molded her body to his. A touch of a smile played around his moon-sculptured lips.

"Are you?" he challenged lazily.

"Yes!"

He slid one hand up to cradle her head, and dipped his head to meet her lips. His movements were slow and deliberate, almost calculated, as if to prove to her that her defenses were no match for his lovemaking expertise.

But something went wrong with his calculations. She felt it in the ragged catch of his breath when their lips met and something raw and primitive ignited between them. No longer was he laughing or teasing, sure in his cool control of the situation. One arm arched her body against his, and the fingers of his other hand tangled in her hair, the harsh grip almost painful. His mouth crushed hers in a savage kiss as uncontrolled as the river raging behind them. His tongue invaded her mouth in hungry exploration, and his hand left her hair to chart the curves of her breast like a conquering invader.

Lark felt tossed and whirled, helpless as an oarless raft caught in the tempestuous power of the river. She fought against the power, fought against surrendering to the unknown riptide that surrounded them, afraid of plunging into depths where she had never ventured before.

And then it was too late and the tide engulfed her. With a little moan her hands crept up behind his neck. No longer did her mouth resist the intimate invasion of his tongue. She welcomed the exploration, reveled in the intoxicating taste of his mouth and the hard male thrust of his body. His hand slid beneath the light cotton blouse and left a burning trail to the aching peak of her breast. She had the heady feeling that deep within her there were unknown senses as yet untouched, poised on the brink of awakening under his relentless advance.

Then he abruptly pulled back. "My God," he muttered hoarsely, his voice remorseful. "I'm no better than Desmond . . ."

"But I'm not running," Lark said softly. She ran her fingers lightly over the sharp angle of his jaw and then lifted herself on tiptoe to bring her lips to his. For a moment he didn't respond, and she knew the plummeting agony of rejection of her tentative, inexperienced advance. Then with a groan he wrapped his arms around her and pulled her to him.

His mouth found hers, and this time his tongue met an eager reception . . . and then a small, experimental dart of answering exploration. No longer was she simply a passive recipient of his kiss and embrace. She met him halfway, eagerly running exploring fingers over the long, sinewy muscles of his back, experiencing with every awakening nerve in her body the intimate feel of his maleness molded against her.

"My little Miss Innocence," Rand groaned softly. "Do you know what you're doing to me?"

"Tell me," she whispered recklessly. She tilted her head to explore the throbbing pulse in his throat with her lips.

"You're setting me on fire." His hand found a way beneath the silken wisp of her bra, and the rough-textured touch of his warm fingertips sent a wave of longing shuddering through her. Her usually softly rounded breasts felt taut and hard, exquisitely sensitive to the soft squeeze of his fingertips. "You bring out the predatory animal in me."

Lark felt one tiny flicker of dismay. The fire of passion . . . the animal throb of desire . . . yes, she felt that too! But the desire she felt was inescapably entwined with the deeper and far more lasting emotion of love.

With a soft growl deep in his throat Rand suddenly swept her up in his arms, and then nothing else mattered but the moment as he kissed her again while he held her suspended weightless in his arms. They met as equals this time, neither invader nor invaded, neither conquerer nor conquered, but with an unleashed blending of passion, of flame recklessly meeting flame to rage higher and higher in a wildfire of desire Lark knew would take more than kisses to quench. . . .

Lark didn't know, hardly dared consider, what would

have happened next if the young guide Benny hadn't come down the trail yelling that Rand was wanted on the telephone. He stopped short in embarrassment when he realized the intimate moment he had interrupted.

Rand hesitated, but Benny muttered that the call was long distance, and finally he set her on her feet. "You're okay now?"

"Yes, I . . . I'm fine." Lark tried to keep a giveaway breathlessness out of her voice. Benny was looking at her with an openly curious expression.

Rand scowled and headed for the lodge with his long strides. Lark lingered a few moments, and then, more slowly, made her way back to the lodge, still a little dazed by what had happened.

She went in the back way, peering tentatively into the living room, where guests were drinking and talking. By that time Rand was off the phone, but a guest had trapped him into repairing a broken camera strap. Lark slipped to her room unnoticed, glad when she reached it that Pam was not there.

Much as she liked her open, cheerful roommate, just now Lark wanted to be alone, though for far different reasons than when she raced away from the repulsive Mr. Desmond. She lay down on the bed fully dressed, her hands crossed behind her head in the darkened room, reliving the wild rapture of Rand's embrace. She ran the tip of her tongue around her mouth, bruised by the untamed violence of Rand's urgent kiss. Shakily she realized that Rand, too, perhaps bore the marks of that kiss, where her fingernails dug into the back of his neck as she returned his kiss with a matching passion. For once, she thought with a certain tremulous satisfaction, Rand's iron self-control seemed to have been shaken. And there had been that angry, almost possessive look on his face when he first caught up with her.

Lark rolled over on her stomach and rested her chin on her cupped hands, wondering what Rand's true feelings were for her. There was no mistaking the passion in his embrace. But Lark, naive as she might seem, was worldly enough to know that neither possessiveness nor passion necessarily meant real love.

But he wasn't just using her to teach Gloria a lesson, she thought fiercely. He couldn't kiss her like that and be totally in love with Gloria!

Next morning Lark waited nervously but expectantly for a word or smile, even a glance of silent communication from Rand, but he was monopolized by guests at breakfast and then busy packing supplies and gear for the trip. From her office desk she could hear the excited chatter of guests milling around waiting for the river trip to begin. Occasionally she could hear Rand's calm authoritative voice giving instructions or answering questions.

If she craned her neck, she could just see him through the office window as he and Benny lifted a heavy food chest into the rear of the pickup. His dark good looks and lean-hipped physique made him stand out in any crowd, but he had more, a vitality, a certain virile magnetism, that went beyond mere good looks.

He stepped back from the loaded pickup and brushed his hands against his Levi's. Everything was evidently ready to be taken down and loaded on the rafts. Lark saw Rand turn and stride toward the rear door of the lodge, and she scrambled for her desk. She didn't intend to be caught craning her head out the window like some infatuated schoolgirl! When Rand came to tell her good-bye, she would be very self-controlled and poised. She was still shaken by the wild abandon with which she had kissed him last night . . . and a little shocked by the deeper, unfamiliar hungers his kiss had aroused in her.

She typed addresses on half a dozen envelopes to be used to mail the checks Mr. Hammond had signed to pay various bills. Where was Rand? He had only to walk down the hallway and through the living room to reach her little office. Someone must have detained him.

She typed a letter Mr. Hammond had dictated to a government agency handling permits on the river.

She was just rereading the letter when she heard a noise from outside. Without a thought for self-control or poise, she dashed to the window. She reached it just in time to see the pickup pulling away, Rand at the wheel. It couldn't be, she thought in dismay. Rand wouldn't leave without saying good-bye to her. Not after last night.

But that was exactly what he was doing.

For a few minutes she held the hope that he planned to return to the lodge before leaving, but that hope sank when Mr. Hammond drove the empty pickup back. Rand was gone without even bothering to tell her good-bye, without even acknowledging by word or smile what had happened between them last night. Somehow his actions seemed to deny that anything *had* happened between them.

No, that couldn't be true, Lark told herself wildly. Rand was simply busy, preoccupied with the responsibilities of the trip. And yet the sinking suspicion lingered that the kiss had not been as earth-shattering for him as it had been for her, that she was making too much of what had been merely a casual interlude in the moonlight.

Chapter Seven

Lark took the typed letter to Mr. Hammond for his signature and then walked up to the main road to leave the letters in the box for the rural mail carrier. In spite of the glorious sunshine, the three days until Rand returned stretched out gloomy and desolate ahead of her, and she felt dull and depressed. She had just started back to the lodge when the mail carrier arrived, and she went back to pick up the mail. She leafed through it idly, surprised to find a letter addressed to her. Inside was a brief, cheerful note from Beth Wyler, plus a bulky letter she had forwarded from the lawyer in Seattle.

Lark opened the second envelope slowly. The letter from the lawyer was concise and businesslike, asking her to sign the enclosed forms and papers so he could finish up her father's tangled estate. At the bottom of the typewritten letter was a handwritten postscript saying that Stanley was upset and worried about her. The lawyer said he had not given Lark's San Diego address to Stanley since their lawyer-client relationship precluded giving out such confidential information, but Stanley was also his personal friend and he hoped Lark might see her way clear to contact Stanley.

Behind the lawyer's rather stilted language Lark sensed his disapproval of the way she had terminated her relationship with Stanley. Perhaps he was right, she thought with a sigh. Perhaps she had been unfair.

She was almost back to the lodge when Gloria, dressed in a brief white tennis outfit, came out of the courts to intercept her. The bright sunlight did not particularly flatter Gloria's skin or hair, giving it a brittle, artificial look, but Lark guiltily realized that she was perhaps looking or hoping for flaws.

"Anything for me?" Gloria asked.

Lark leafed through the bundle of envelopes and advertisements again. "I don't see anything."

Gloria shrugged, and Lark had the feeling Gloria hadn't really been expecting anything and had something else on her mind. Gloria swung the tennis racket lightly over her shoulder. "That was quite a little exhibition you and Rand put on last night," she remarked.

Lark felt her face flame in embarrassment and astonishment. But her momentary sense of shame was suddenly dispelled by a fiercely defiant joy that Gloria *had* seen the passionate embrace. It should certainly have made clear to Gloria that Rand's attentions to Lark were more than some pretense to teach Gloria a lesson.

"It was really very effective," Gloria went on reflectively. "Moonlight glittering on the water, the two of you standing out on the rocky point practically glued to each other. Very convincing."

"If what you're saying is that Rand wasn't ashamed to be seen kissing me, then I must say I . . . I'm glad!" Lark said recklessly. "Because I'm not ashamed of it either!"

Gloria laughed. "Of course he wasn't ashamed. He deliberately arranged a time and place when he was sure he *would* be seen." Her voice was condescending. "He fully intended that I see the whole show. It was part of the plan to teach me a lesson."

"That isn't true!" Lark gasped. It couldn't be. It was she who had raced headlong to the river. Rand had done nothing to arrange that.

"Isn't it?" Gloria lifted her dark eyebrows. "How do you think I happened to see it all, then? By pure chance? Don't be naive. Rand and I had been strolling around the grounds with that older couple from New York. We stopped and sat on the benches under the oaks to watch the moon. After we were almost back to the lodge, the wife realized she had left her cashmere shawl on the bench. I went back to get it for her."

"But I don't see how you can say Rand planned . . . I mean . . ." Lark's protest trailed off doubtfully.

"Would you care to come to the bench with me and see exactly what a fine view it has of the rocky point where Rand staged his little exhibition?" Gloria challenged.

Lark clutched the bundle of letters, her hands damp. Rand couldn't have planned the "exhibition" quite as deliberately as Gloria suggested. There were too many elements of chance involved. But he could very well have decided to take advantage of the situation just in case Gloria was watching at the right moment.

Gloria sighed. "When Rand feels I have been properly chastised, he'll come back to me." She shook her cloud of dark hair. "I suppose I should be angry with him, but his motives are so transparent. If men only knew how easily we women can see through them!"

Gloria probably could see through men, Lark thought dismally. But Lark herself was too blinded by love to see anything clearly.

"I do hope I haven't upset you," Gloria said suddenly, her voice solicitously saccharine. "I warned you that Rand would have no compunction about using you for his own purposes. He can be quite ruthless, I'm afraid."

Lark didn't reply. She just fled inside the lodge, stopping only to dump the mail on the office desk before seeking refuge in her own room. She paced back and forth between the bunk beds, her chest rising and falling in agitation. She didn't want to believe anything Gloria had said, and yet it *was* all so terribly believable. Of all the times Rand might have chosen to kiss her, why had it happened in full view of Gloria unless that was exactly when Rand wanted it to happen?

The argument went on within her. There was Rand's obvious passion when he kissed her. Was that only pretended? No, she couldn't believe that. But it didn't necessarily mean the same thing to him that it did to her.

Perhaps most damning of all was Gloria's own attitude toward what had happened. If Gloria had any suspicion at all that Rand had any *real* interest in Lark, Lark was positive Gloria would be furious. There would be none of this calm, amused air of patience if Gloria suspected Rand was beginning to care for Lark.

The fact that Gloria was not even angry seemed to say it all. Lark had the unhappy feeling that the smartest thing she could do right now would be to pack up and get out, no matter how slim the contents of her purse might be. She had recognized earlier that she was already in love with Rand. His passionate kiss had only deepened her feelings for him. But now she had the sinking feeling that the longer she stayed, the more agonizing her heartbreak would be. And yet, even as she was thinking that, she knew she couldn't tear herself away now. She was already in too deep.

The three days until Lark made the trip in the van to pick up the guests at the end of the river trip dragged out endlessly. She felt listless and dispirited. She did accomplish one thing, however. She decided the lawyer and Rand were right. She had treated Stanley unfairly. She wrote a long letter explaining everything as best she could, telling him where she was and what she was doing, that she was happy and everything was fine. That wasn't the total truth, but she felt it would serve to make Stanley feel better. Her conscience felt better also when the letter was done. She mailed the letter to Stanley at the same time she returned the signed forms to the lawyer, and promptly forgot both in her greater concern over her feelings for Rand.

She kept thinking that when she saw Rand again, something would happen and she would know for certain how he really felt about her. The suspense would end.

But nothing so definitive happened. When she drove into the rocky parking area at Foster Bar, the rafts were already beached and waiting. Rand was courteous but distant, as if his mind were elsewhere. She hoped he would seek her out and talk to her, but instead he left the lodge the same day with no more than a preoccupied nod in her direction. If anyone knew where he had gone, Lark was not informed, and she had too much pride to ask.

Rand returned to the lodge late the following afternoon, as uncommunicative as when he left. Some minor problem with the jet boat had developed, and he went down to the dock immediately to take a look at the engine.

Lark had just finished registering some new guests when the telephone rang. It was a call for the young guide Benny from his girlfriend. Lark pushed the office window open and called to Benny as he was climbing into the pickup.

"Benny, Chrissy is on the phone."

Benny groaned. "I can't talk to her now. Rand is waiting for me to bring these rafts down to the river. And you know how Rand feels about waiting."

Benny was obviously torn, wanting to talk to his girlfriend but wary of annoying Rand. He looked at Lark appealingly, as if she should be able to solve his problem.

Lark hesitated. She was through in the office for the day. "Would you like me to take the rafts down to Rand?" she asked finally.

Benny beamed. He was already headed toward the extension phone in the kitchen when he called over his shoulder, "Thanks, Lark. You're terrific!"

Lark immediately began regretting her offer of help.

Rand had obviously been avoiding her. Or, if not actually avoiding her, was showing himself indifferent to her existence. Perhaps it was she, as well as Gloria, whom Rand was teaching a lesson, Lark thought unhappily. A lesson in the dangers of recklessly falling in love.

Lark had not driven the lodge pickup before, but the gear positions were marked and she had no problems. The loaded trailer clattered along behind. Rand made a sweeping circular motion with his hand as she approached the concrete boat ramp. When she braked, not understanding the gesture, he impatiently motioned again.

She poked her head out the window. "I'm sorry, I don't understand what you want." She kept her voice crisp and impersonal.

He glanced up sharply, evidently not realizing until that moment that it was Lark and not Benny driving. He walked toward her, eyes narrowing. "What are you doing here?"

Lark explained briefly.

Rand scowled, obviously annoyed with the complications of Benny's young love life. "I would think Benny's girlfriend could time her calls so they did not interrupt his work and inconvenience everyone else," he muttered.

Lark was suddenly reminded of another urgent, interrupting phone call, and from a change in Rand's expression she realized he was remembering it also.

After a long pause he finally said, "The call was from my mother. She hadn't heard from my grandfather for a while and was concerned about him. He has a heart problem."

"Oh. I didn't know. I'm sorry," Lark said awkwardly. "You went to see him?"

"No. If he wants me, he knows where to reach me." Rand's voice held a stubborn, angry note. Sounding almost reluctant, he added finally, "I did talk to his doctor, however. He's concerned too."

"Perhaps the strain of running the company is too much for your grandfather," Lark ventured.

"It's his choice," Rand said harshly. He abruptly changed the subject. "You'll have to turn the pickup around and back the trailer toward the ramp."

He turned and walked away before Lark had time to protest that she had never before backed a vehicle with a trailer attached. He made the impatient circular gesture again, which she now realized was meant to show her where to turn and back the trailer.

She put the pickup in gear and started turning in as tight a circle as possible. There was insufficient room to turn completely around, and she had to maneuver backward and forward several times. Finally the pickup was turned around, with the trailer headed toward the river. Lark's hands were damp with nervous perspiration, but she thought she had accomplished the hardest part of the task.

She was wrong.

Backing the trailer toward the boat ramp looked as if it should be a simple task. Rand had made it look easy the time she watched him back the big jet-boat trailer into the water. All she had to do was keep the pickup and trailer going in a straight line.

But the obstinate trailer carrying the three stacked rafts would *not* go in a straight line. It twisted to the right, then to the left. The trailer tongue creaked ominously under the strain. Her neck ached with the effort of craning her head around, trying to see where she was going.

Finally Rand strode up to the window. "I take it you've never backed a trailer before," he commented laconically.

"I'm doing the best I can," Lark snapped.

"If you're going to drive for the lodge, then it's time you learned to back a trailer properly."

"And I suppose you're going to teach me!" Lark flared, frustrated and annoyed at her own failure and angry at his superior attitude. "Teaching people lessons seems to be what you like to do best!"

Rand had reached through the open window to grasp the steering wheel with one hand, and he paused to look at her, eyes appraising. His lean, strong features were only a few inches from hers, his skin already tan from the hours spent on the river, and her own skin prickled with a sensual awareness of his nearness. "And just what do you mean by that?" he asked. His voice had an ominous calm.

"You know what I mean," Lark said evasively. When his intent, piercing gaze did not falter, she added defensively, "But you and your grandfather are probably both too stubborn for either of you to ever learn any lesson!"

Rand's chiseled jaw tightened. "I've told you before. You know nothing about the situation and are not in a position to judge."

"I know enough about the situation with Gloria to judge!" The words were out before Lark could stop them, and she instantly regretted them.

"Would you care to explain that?" he asked in that same ominous tone that made Lark flutter inside. When she didn't answer, he added harshly, "I take it you and Mrs. Quigley have been gossiping again."

"No! I mean . . . Everyone knows you were in love with Gloria but she threw you over for another man. Now you're trying to get even with her and teach her a lesson."

"By doing what?" he challenged.

"Pretending to be interested in me! By . . . by kissing me where she had to see!"

"Do you really think I have nothing better to do with my time than play adolescent games?" he demanded contemptuously.

Uncertainly Lark caught her tremulous lower lip between her teeth. Was it possible Gloria was wrong about Rand's motives? Or that she was deliberately trying to cause trouble between Lark and Rand, intending to take advantage of the tension and suspicion she caused? Lark certainly wouldn't put such a devious trick past Gloria, of course. And yet Rand hadn't actually denied the accusations; he had merely passed them off as being beneath serious consideration.

"Now, if you'd care to learn how to back a trailer properly, I'll be happy to teach you," Rand stated coolly, arrogantly dismissing her accusations as if they were of no consequence.

Lark hesitated and finally nodded. Reaching through the window, Rand showed her how to position her hands on the wheel for best control, which way to turn the steering wheel when she wanted the trailer to go right or left, how to alter direction only slightly so as not to overcorrect and turn the trailer too far in the opposite direction. His strong hands occasionally brushed hers as he spoke, and she found his nearness distracting.

Finally he stepped back. "Think you can do it now?"

"I'll try."

She kept her eyes on the rearview mirror as he instructed, instead of awkwardly craning her neck around to see. At first everything went fine. He stood to the rear, motioning her which way to go. Then the trailer suddenly angled off to the left, for no particular reason that she could ascertain. She turned the wheel as Rand had instructed, and the trailer responded by cutting too sharply in the other direction. The trailer seemed to have a totally contrary will of its own. Lark fought back tears of frustration.

"You're overcorrecting," he called. "You'll have to pull ahead and straighten out. Don't get excited."

"I am not getting excited," Lark called back, her denial belied by the reflection of her flushed face in the rearview mirror. She jerked the pickup forward and started backing again. And again the trailer angled off to one side.

"No, you have to start with the wheels straight," Rand called. "Then turn the steering wheel just *slightly*."

By now the sun had dropped behind the forested mountains and the air was cool, but Lark's shirt clung damply to her back and little beads of perspiration trickled between her breasts. Her hair persisted in falling in her eyes, and her hands were cramped from gripping the steering wheel so tightly. The seat was set too far back for her, and her legs ached from straining to reach the pedals. Rand's careful instructions melted into an incomprehensible jumble. She was tired and sweaty and uncomfortable, and Rand's last bit of advice was suddenly too much for her. She jerked the emergency brake on and shoved the door open.

"Since I can't seem to do it to suit you, why don't you just back the trailer yourself," she snapped.

He lifted a dark eyebrow. "Running away from an unpleasant situation again, I see," he observed.

"I am not running away!" Lark stormed. Tears of anger and frustration stung her eyes as she realized her protest was hardly convincing when she already had one foot on the ground. He just stood there, an infuriating, taunting smile on his lips. Furiously she slammed back into the pickup and released the brake.

Then, carefully as a tightrope walker balancing on a high wire, she backed the pickup and trailer toward the ramp, resolutely correcting the steering wheel only a fraction of an inch at a time in response to Rand's signals to angle to the right or left. Finally he held up his palm to signal her to a stop. He smiled approvingly as she got out to inspect the completed task.

"Good job. I knew you could do it if you'd just stick to it."

Rand's approval was gratifying, but Lark's sudden surge of elation and satisfaction with herself for what she had accomplished went even deeper. The trailer wasn't perfectly positioned on the boat ramp, but it was close enough that the rafts would have to be hand-carried only a few feet to the water. It was the kind of difficult task she might have given up on not so very long ago.

Would probably have given up on today, she had to admit to herself, if Rand hadn't infuriated her into sticking to it.

But she could do it again if she had to, she thought exultantly. And better and faster the next time!

Lark was so busy congratulating herself that she jumped when she felt a hand touch the back of her neck.

"Relax," Rand said. "Your muscles are all tied up in nervous knots." He stood behind her, both hands gently massaging the taut muscles of her neck and shoulders. "You did fine. I suppose you'll be wanting to learn to run the jet boat next."

"I might." Her thoughts had a reckless defiance, but the words came out shakily. Her tongue didn't seem to be working quite right. The touch of his fingertips loosened the taut muscles, but at the same time sent shivery tingles shooting through her.

"You're a fast learner. But then, as you've pointed out, I'm very good at teaching people lessons, so perhaps I deserve part of the credit." The words were more teasing than taunting, and his voice was a husky caress that blended with the mesmerizing touch of his fingers. She stood there feeling the nervous tension drain away under his expert touch, only to be replaced by something infinitely more disturbing. His hands slipped down to hold her waist and his lips brushed the curve of her throat. She tilted her head back, eyes half-closed, as his mouth and hands continued to send wordless messages tingling through her. She could feel the length of his lean, hard body against her back.

Lark's mind and body felt drugged by the caresses of his voice and mouth and hands. His lips tantalized her earlobe, and his hands once again found bare skin beneath her blouse. The wild thought occurred to her that there was more that he could teach her, much, much more, and it had nothing at all to do with trailers or jet boats. . . . She turned in his arms, mouth lifted to meet his in an overpowering rush of eagerness to be taught.

But before her parted lips met his, she was suddenly aware of laughter and voices on the trail. Her eyes flew open and she jerked away from him, startled as much by her reckless reaction to his caresses as by the interruption. She stared at him, eyes wide, heart thundering.

Rand glanced toward the trail as several people emerged from the trees. There was the hint of a scowl on his face. "We never seem to manage to be alone for long, do we?" he commented wryly. He seemed calm, but a betraying pulse throbbed in his throat.

"Do you . . . want to be alone with me?" Lark asked rashly.

"Let's go into town and have dinner together tonight."

"I didn't mean . . . I wasn't hinting . . ." Lark felt flustered. Then she took a deep breath. Maybe she had been hinting! "I'd like that," she finally said simply.

Rand unhooked the trailer and drove the pickup back to the lodge. Lark's mind was spinning around a carousel of thoughts about where they would go and what she would wear. Benny, looking a little sheepish, hung up the kitchen phone just as they walked inside. It rang almost the moment he set it down.

The call was for Rand. Lark handed the phone to him and went on through to the office to cover her typewriter. Rand's face had a taut, controlled expression when he caught up with her a minute later.

"My grandfather has just been taken to the hospital. Possible heart attack."

"Oh, Rand, how terrible!" Quickly she added, "We'll have dinner some other time."

"No. I want you to come with me." His voice was decisive, though his thoughts seemed to be elsewhere. "We'll eat later, after we go to the hospital."

Lark glanced down at her clothes. She was wearing what she usually wore in the informal atmosphere of the lodge, jeans and a simple short-sleeved blouse, but there

obviously was no time to change. Rand was already
striding toward the door. She took a moment to tell Mrs.
Hammond she was leaving, grabbed a sweater, and followed Rand to his pickup. She didn't know why Rand
wanted her along in this time of crisis, but if he needed
her, nothing was more important than being with him.

Rand was silent on the ride into town, grim and preoccupied. Once they arrived at the hospital, they went
immediately into the emergency waiting room together.
Rand asked about his grandfather and then disappeared
with a nurse down a hallway. Lark took one of the seats
lined up along the wall. The hospital had a sharp, medic-
inal smell that was a sickening reminder to Lark of other
times she had spent in hospitals, times that had ended
tragically. She had never met Rand's grandfather, had
never heard anything but unflattering comments about
him, but she felt a strong sense of compassion for him.
And for Rand too. In spite of his bitter differences with
his grandfather, it was obvious Rand was deeply concerned about the elderly man.

Rand was not gone long. He said nothing when he returned, and Lark wondered uneasily if he was regretting
his impulse to bring her along. Outside, he sat in the
pickup with hands clenched around the steering wheel,
dark eyes staring unseeingly into the deepening dusk.

"It's all my fault," he said bitterly. "He wouldn't be
lying in there now if it weren't for me."

"Is he . . . very bad?"

"The doctors are running some tests now. They're
supposed to call me later with the results. Or if there is
any change in his condition."

"Is there anything I can do?"

He smiled grimly. "Maybe give me a good swift kick
for being so stubborn." He paused. "Once you accused
me of running out on my responsibilities to my grandfather and the company. You were right. I should have
tried harder to see his point of view. Or tried harder to

make him understand mine. We could have worked out some compromise if I hadn't been so stubborn."

"You mustn't blame yourself." Impulsively Lark reached out and touched his hand. "This might have happened anyway."

"And it might not have. He might have gone on for years, cantankerous and grumbling, but alive and well, if he hadn't been under the strain of running the company alone."

There was nothing more Lark could say, and all she could do was give his hand another sympathetic squeeze.

"We'd better get something to eat," Rand said. He sounded as if it were an obligation rather than something he wanted to do.

"I'm really not dressed to go anywhere." Lark self-consciously ran her fingers over the denim material, though her self-consciousness came not so much from what she was wearing as from a feeling that she was intruding at a private time.

Rand glanced at her as if suddenly seeing her for the first time. "You couldn't look more beautiful to me if you were wearing satin and diamonds," he said huskily. Unexpectedly he tilted her chin up and brushed her lips lightly with a kiss. "But I had in mind picking up something and taking it to the house to eat. The hospital is supposed to telephone me there, and I don't want to miss their call."

"Your grandfather's house?"

Rand shook his head, and Lark remembered now that Mrs. Quigley had once mentioned Rand had a house in town, a house that Mrs. Quigley thought needed "a wife and a passel of kids." Rand didn't explain now why he and his grandfather, each a man alone, had separate homes, but Lark didn't really need to be told. Each was too fiercely independent, too determined to do things his own way. But Rand, she also knew, was willing now to compromise. She fervently hoped it wasn't already too late for that.

They went by a Chinese restaurant, picked up a take-out dinner, and then drove through town and up a long winding private road to Rand's house on a ridge over-looking town. The automatic garage doors opened with a flick of Rand's hand on the controls inside the pickup. Inside the basement garage was another car, a sleek silvery-blue Porsche. Stairs led up to the main level of the house. Lark gave a small gasp of delight when she saw the view from the cathedral windows. The lights of the town were spread out below, circled by the dark silhou-ettes of mountains, and above was the splendor of the starry skies.

Rand built a fire in the fireplace while Lark opened the cartons of food and heated water for tea in the spacious, well-equipped kitchen. The unoccupied house was chilly, and they ate on the myrtlewood coffee table near the crackling fire. Afterward they watched the moon rise over the mountains, the golden globe hovering for a few minutes like a giant ball rolling down the angle of a forested slope. But instead of rolling, it soared into the night sky, lost its golden glow, and turned silver-white.

Rand had set the telephone on the edge of the coffee table near the fireplace, but it remained stubbornly silent. How long would they have to wait before the hospital called, before Rand had some idea of his grandfather's fate? Rand asked a few casual questions about Lark's growing-up years, and she sensed he wanted to talk about something, anything, to keep his mind from dwell-ing on the morbid possibilities.

Rand stretched out on the carpet in front of the fire-place and she sat on the raised hearth, talking at random of years gone by. Finally he responded by talking of his own childhood, always at odds with his dictatorial grandfather, and yet sharing a deep bond of affection with him. When he rose to replenish the fire with wood, Lark moved out of the way and sat cross-legged on the carpet.

He returned to sit beside her, and they stared into the dancing flames together.

"I'm glad you're here with me," Rand said huskily. "It makes the waiting bearable. You've come a long way from the scared, uncertain girl I rescued on a mountain road a while back," he added unexpectedly.

He tipped her chin up and kissed her lightly. But something happened. It was as if the kiss was a spark, a spark that landed on something explosively flammable. It flared between them as their eyes caught and held, hers blue and wide and uncertain, his dark and suddenly smoldering. Then his mouth returned to hers in a kiss of such depth and intensity that Lark felt strangely disoriented, as if she soared with that silver-white moon across the night sky.

Her eyes were closed, but still she saw the dancing flames and jeweled stars . . . or were the flames and stars within herself? Unresistingly she slid to the lush carpet beneath the hard crush of his body. Her arms crept around his neck, and her hands tangled in his crisp hair. His lips explored her face and throat, lingered on her closed eyelids, and whispered tantalizingly at the corners of her lips until she turned her mouth to his in fierce demand. Unfamiliar hungers stirred within her, tentatively at first, then with increasing strength and boldness. The small sound she made as his lips found the upper curve of her breast was more pleasure than protest, even though some small part of her mind signaled frantic warnings.

And then the telephone shrilled.

Rand tensed but didn't move. Then, almost reluctantly, as if half-angry at the interruption even though he had been waiting for the call, he reached for the phone. His body was still half over hers, molded intimately to her curves and hollows, as he talked on the phone. One hand lingered on her breast as if loath to leave it.

The words he spoke into the phone were indistinct

murmurs to Lark as the blood still pounded in her veins. She studied the lock of hair falling across his tanned forehead, rested her fingertips against the pulse throbbing in his throat, reveled in the hard, intimate press of his body. Little Miss Innocence, he had teasingly called her more than once: But her roaming thoughts and burgeoning desires now were anything but innocent. This was the man she loved, she thought with a kind of wonder. Strong, ruggedly masculine, commanding—sometimes infuriatingly so!—but gentle and caring, too.

He returned the phone to the coffee table, and she read the flood of relief in his eyes.

"He's all right?"

"More or less. He's already grumbling that it was just a touch of indigestion and this is a big fuss over nothing." Rand's mouth twitched in a smile at this all-too-predictable reaction from his grandfather. "But no matter what he says, the doctor says it was a heart attack, and he's going to have to take it easy."

"I'm glad he's going to be all right," Lark said honestly. She made a tentative move to sit up, but he slid over her, imprisoning her beneath the solid length of his body. His hands framed her face as his eyes studied her. "I . . . I should be getting back to the lodge . . ." She faltered.

"Do you want to go?" His fingertips traced the line of her jaw and then his mouth found hers in a kiss that was achingly sweet.

Want to go? Her senses spun dreamily. She wanted nothing more than to be where she was right now, lost in his arms, drifting in his kisses.

"Do you know I find your mouth irresistible?" He touched the softness of her mouth with his. "Even when you're yelling at me about some little thing like a trailer that won't back straight, I find I'm thinking about kissing you." The small hint of laughter in his voice deepened to huskiness.

Her fingers twined softly around the slight curl where

his crisp dark hair met his tanned neck. "And what are you thinking about now?" she asked tremulously.

"I'm thinking I want to make love to you."

She knew it, and yet to hear him say it brought a heavy, expectant thud to her heartbeat. She wanted it too! She loved him. Every muscle and nerve within her cried out for physical fulfillment of that love, and yet at the same time she felt strangely shy and achingly vulnerable, precariously insecure as she hovered on the edge of the unknown.

"Rand, I don't know. I . . ." She caught her lower lip, lush and full from his sensuous kisses, between her teeth. "I . . . I've never . . ."

"I know." He brushed a strand of hair from her forehead. Her face had a flushed glow that came from the smolder of desire growing between them rather than the warmth of the flames dancing nearby. "Do you like to have me hold you?"

"Yes . . ."

"And kiss you?" His mouth met hers, gently at first, then with an increasing sweet, possessive depth that left her breathless.

"Oh, yes . . ." she breathed softly, eyes still closed.

He kissed her almost translucent eyelids, and she made no sound of protest when he lifted and carried her down a darkened hallway. The bedroom glowed softly with moonlight spilling through the windows, creating charcoal shadows and pools of silver. He set her gently on one of the shadows, and she felt the soft fluff of a pillow beneath her head.

She felt a dreamy sense of inevitability, but when he knelt over her and unfastened the top button of her blouse, her fingers instinctively closed over his hand to stop him.

"I want to touch you," he whispered softly. "I want you to touch me."

Still kneeling over her, he removed his own shirt, and in the soft moonglow his skin gleamed. Tentatively, almost wonderingly, she ran her fingertips over the skin just above his belt. It felt smooth but hard with the strength of underlying muscle.

His hands moved down the row of buttons, slowly at first, not wanting to alarm her, then with growing urgency. When he reached the clasp of her bra, his hands, though not uncertain, were strangely less deft than usual, as if the glory of the treasure he was about to expose had affected his coordination. When the clasp finally fell free, she felt more than heard the soft catch of his breath as he gazed down at her.

"Now I know it is not only your mouth I find irresistible," he whispered huskily. Against the dark shadow of the bed, her naked skin had a pearly, almost luminescent glow. His fingertips stroked her breasts with a touch as light and flickering as dancing firelight. She felt the rosy tips rise and harden under his touch, as if seeking to follow the elusive caress that advanced and retreated maddeningly. A small, yearning murmur escaped her throat as her body arched toward him longingly, and finally, at last, his hand encompassed the full rounded globe.

"See?" he said softly. "You like that too."

"Yes, oh yes . . ." She lay back, limp, her senses softly spinning as she felt the satisfying fullness of the gently squeezing caress.

Then the same tantalizing process began all over again, except on an exquisitely higher plane as his tongue bewitched her breasts in a way even his masterful hands could not, touching her taut nipples with tiny flickers and darts of sweet fire. The feeling was a strange, sweet torture, like being offered an exquisitely tempting delicacy and then having it snatched away before she could grab it. She reached for it again and again, arching and twisting her body to catch the tantalizing caress, until she could stand it no more. With a cry of pure demand she tangled her hands in his hair and held him to her. She felt his deep rumble of satisfaction that echoed her own when his mouth encompassed the yielding globe of her breast almost as fully as his hand had.

When he finally lifted his head, he asked softly, "Do you still have any doubts?"

His voice drifted to Lark from somewhere far away, like a softly falling leaf. She ran the palms of her hands over the long, tautly curved muscles of his back. Doubt? True, overwhelming desire, desire that surpassed all sense of reason and control, was something Lark had always faintly doubted existed. But she doubted it no more. It hovered on the horizon of her existence, swept toward her as inexorably as a storm cloud.

And then the storm broke around them. With an almost frantic haste, Rand stripped the remaining clothing from her body, and her fumbling eager hands helped remove his. He knelt within the silken triangle of her thighs, his hands softly stroking the warm skin. In the shadowy moonlight Lark could not see his eyes and yet she could feel his gaze caressing her body, taking pleasure in each swelling curve and hollow. She ran her fingertips over his hard-muscled thighs and gloried in the pure animal magnificence of his male body. Tentatively her fingers traced the tan line across his flat abdomen and then boldly explored the unknown territory of untanned skin below.

She felt the faint tremor of his reaction, but still he waited for her to make the final surrender. She made it willingly. With a small cry she lifted her arms and he came into them, swiftly but gently covering her willing body with the lean length of his. Lark knew one brief moment of the physical resistance of her own inexperienced body, but the muffled sound she made was more surprise than pain, and then her senses were opened to the joyous potential of her full womanhood as he taught her the unknown secrets of her own body.

So many new and incredible delights. The feel of the full, hard length of his body against hers, with no barrier between them . . . the faint musky scent of the blended heat of their bodies . . . the small wordless sounds of pleasure and need, desire and surrender, that were more meaningful than spoken words. Even his mouth had a new and heady taste as he kissed her while his body loved her. She had a sense of complete and total oneness as they moved together toward a height she had never been more than dimly aware existed, like a light that beckoned her upward. And when she reached it, the light exploded in a shower of tender violence around her. . . .

"Are you the goddess of my river?" he whispered. A soft sheen of perspiration glistened on his forehead in the moonlight. He rested his head against hers. "So deep and serene . . . and then wild and tempestuous in my arms . . . but I never want to tame you, just be with you. . . ."

Did she fall asleep? Or did she only drift on a dreamy cloud of rapture, reluctant to come back to earth? She lay on her side now, Rand's body curved warmly around hers. Full moonlight had reached the bed. She felt luminous as the silvery light—but a good deal more warm and earthy and satisfied. Rand lay with his head supported on one hand as he looked down at her, his hand sliding in a long, possessive caress along the curve of her hip.

"I don't think I gave you a chance to answer my question about whether or not you wanted to go," he said softly.

Her answer was simple and direct. "This was my answer."

Still he lay looking down at her as the moonlight gilded the fan of her hair against the pillow. "Why are you watching me?" she asked wonderingly, suddenly almost uneasy.

"Maybe I'm afraid if I go to sleep I'll wake up and you won't be here."

Her momentary unease melted as she turned into the snug harbor of his arms. "I'll be here," she promised. *Always*, she added to herself as she drifted down the comfortable path of sleep, safe and secure in his solid embrace. Forever and always. . . .

She woke to find him slipping out of bed and tucking the covers around her. Her eyes struggled open. The magic moonlight had been replaced by gray daylight filtering through an overcast sky.

"Go back to sleep." His lips brushed her temple. "The doctor said he'd be at the hospital about seven this morning, and I want to meet him there. I'll bring back something for breakfast later."

With another brush of his lips against her cheek, he was gone. She heard the sound of the garage doors opening and the pickup leaving. She lay in bed for another ten minutes, but she couldn't go back to sleep. Without Rand the bed felt big and empty, and her naked body was cold without his warmth. There was something else too, something that made her uneasy, though she couldn't quite put her finger on it. She finally attributed it to the effect of the gray, overcast sky. This week's river trip just might get wet. She dressed, wandered out to the kitchen, found coffee and an electric pot.

When the coffee had perked, she poured a cup and stood drinking it at the kitchen counter, letting her mind wander over the magic of last night, savoring Rand's masterful lovemaking. She returned to the bedroom to straighten the bed, stifling an urge to peer curiously into closets and drawers. She did make a quick tour of the house, finding it spacious and quietly elegant. One of the bathrooms had an enormous sunken tub and a stained-glass skylight. There was a recreation room off the basement garage, complete with pool table, bar, and another fireplace.

Her tour of the house complete, Lark restlessly poured another cup of coffee. Where was Rand? What about the river trip he was scheduled to leave with around noon? And how was she going to explain her own overnight absence? She had deliberately put that thought out of her mind last night.

She had just decided she would have to call the lodge when she heard the pickup pull into the garage below. Rand bounded up the stairs carrying a fragrant bakery bag. He looked rugged and vital and happy. He gave her a kiss that was more exuberant than passionate.

"You made coffee? Great! I'm starved."

"How is your grandfather?"

Rand grinned. "Back to his usual grumpy self. But we worked out some compromises. Have you called the lodge? They must be wondering where we are."

When Lark shook her head, Rand dialed from the kitchen phone. Who would answer? Lark wondered. That was usually her job.

Lark couldn't tell who was on the other end of the line as Rand gave a brief explanation of his grandfather's condition. Then the person evidently asked about Lark, because he said, "Yes, she's with me." A pause. "It was too late to return to the lodge last night." Another pause and a darkening scowl. "That really isn't any of your business, Gloria." Another gap of silence; then Rand said, "Yes, I suppose there's room."

Gloria! Lark groaned to herself. How had *she* happened to answer the phone? Not by accident, Lark suddenly suspected. And what had Gloria asked? "Room" for what?

Rand's expression was unreadable as he drank coffee and rapidly ate two of the rolls he had brought. Lark nibbled on one. She would have liked to sit and talk, to consider what had happened between them, but there was no time. Rand had to make several more business phone calls. He was obviously already gathering in the controlling reins of the company again, and she felt oddly left out and abandoned. As if, she thought unhappily as she watched him cradle the phone between ear and shoulder while he scribbled figures on a notepad, last night hadn't been important at all.

He was preoccupied with his own thoughts on the

drive out to the lodge, but as they pulled into the yard he suddenly seemed to become aware of her again.

"I'm sorry," he said suddenly, his voice contrite. "This wasn't fair to you at all, rushing you around like this. But I'm caught in the middle here. I can't walk out on the Hammonds with the river-running season just getting into high gear. Benny's coming along fine as a guide, but he's not experienced enough to take over yet. I'll have to stay until they can replace me. But I have to run the company too."

Rand's brief explanation made Lark feel better. Of course his thoughts were preoccupied. He had a double load of responsibility now. She nodded slowly. His hand slid beneath the golden curtain of her hair and caressed her lightly.

"We'll—"

But she never knew what he started to say, because just then Gloria burst through the lodge door. Her glance darted from Rand's face to Lark's, and Lark had the scarlet feeling that what had happened last night was openly displayed on her face. Her mouth had a full, ripe feeling from Rand's kisses that she was certain would not escape Gloria's stinging glance.

"Benny and Jerry have already hauled most of the supplies down to the rafts," Gloria said. Lark had the sudden feeling Gloria was making a deliberate point of not even mentioning last night.

"What made you decide to go along on this river run?" Rand asked. He sounded oddly suspicious. "A rather sudden decision, wasn't it?"

So that was it. Gloria had asked if there was room on this river trip for her to go along.

"A couple of the guests are friends of mine from San Francisco. I just decided I wanted to spend a little more time with them," Gloria answered.

Gloria's explanation was reasonable enough, and yet Lark knew instinctively that Gloria's reason for going along on the trip had more to do with Rand than any friends from San Francisco. Gloria knew very well that Rand and Lark had spent last night together. Unexpectedly Lark also realized the information was safe with Gloria. Gloria was not about to spread around the fact that the man she was in love with had spent the night making love to another woman.

"I also thought that perhaps you and I would have time to talk when you weren't so . . . busy." Gloria's eyes flicked meaningfully to Lark.

"Maybe you're right." The tilt of Rand's head was thoughtful. "You and I should have a long talk."

Lark sat there feeling as if she had suddenly become invisible, the passion and tenderness of last night made meaningless. She was nothing but a pawn in their volatile game of love. Last night was no different from the kiss by the river—all done for Gloria's benefit, all done to teach her never again to trifle with his love.

With a stricken cry, Lark suddenly thrust the pickup door open and fled.

Chapter Eight

Lark was grateful that the next few days were busy ones. Nothing could keep Lark's thoughts away from her unwanted role in what Gloria had referred to as Rand's "plan" to chastise her, but at least Lark was busy. Mr. Hammond sent her on an all-day trip into town to have repairs made on the van. She went on a jet-boat ride. There were a few minutes of tense excitement when a guest tried to swim across the river, underestimated the power of the current, and had to be rescued.

But all the time, in spite of that last shattering scene before the river trip departed, Lark was dismally aware that she was only marking time until Rand returned, that without him the days were pointless and lackluster. In the back of her mind there was just one small thought that kept her from sinking into total despair. Surely Rand couldn't have made love to her with such sweet, fiery passion unless he felt something for her . . . could he?

In spite of that hope, when Lark drove the van down to Foster Bar to pick up the guests after the river run, she braced herself for the more likely possibility that Rand and Gloria had reconciled, that she would have to see them looking at each other with love in their eyes.

However, that did not appear to be the case, Lark realized, perplexed, as she heard Rand snap a curt reply to a question Gloria asked him. His face had a set, angry expression. Had something gone wrong with their "talk"? Lark wondered, guiltily hopeful.

But on the drive home, Lark realized with a sinking heart that there was another explanation for Rand's stiff aloofness toward Gloria. Gloria and her friends from San Francisco sat directly behind Lark in the van, discussing the river run. Lark gathered that one of the guests, a distinguished-looking businessman from Ohio, had evidently paid Gloria a bit too much attention to suit Rand. One of the girls warned that Gloria was playing with fire encouraging the other man's attentions when Rand was around, but Gloria just laughed blithely and said a little competition kept a man interested. Lark's own bleak private thought was that Gloria's actions were a small warning to Rand that he was going too far in his involvement with Lark, that she would put up with only so many of his "lessons." It was all just another calculated move in their sophisticated game of hearts.

There was the usual flurry of excitement when the van reached the lodge and people collected their belongings and exchanged promises to keep in touch. Lark smiled mechanically, found a misplaced pair of sneakers, obligingly snapped a photo of two couples arm-in-arm with Rand. She was just stepping back into the van to drive it around to the parking area when she heard her name called.

Lark turned unwillingly, presuming the caller was one of the guests demanding something else, but her eyes widened as she saw the unexpected but familiar figure walking toward her. She blinked unbelievingly. It couldn't be . . . but it was.

"Stanley!" Lark gasped. His gray suit and white shirt looked out of place among the casually rumpled, sunburned guests.

"I came as soon as I could rearrange my schedule after

I received your letter," he said. He was smiling a little uncertainly.

Lark couldn't think what to say, and she stared at him in dismay. This wasn't what she had intended at all when she wrote that long letter of explanation to him. Finally she managed to murmur, "This is such a . . . a surprise!"

"You're looking wonderful. All tanned and healthy." He put his hands lightly on her shoulders. "But I don't think you're any too happy to see me."

Lark's natural courtesy prevented her from agreeing aloud with that statement. "It's just that I really am so surprised," she repeated helplessly.

"You should have known I'd come," he reproved gently. "I love you, you know."

"Stanley, I . . . I tried to explain everything in my letter. I'll always think of you as one of the best friends I've ever had, but . . ."

Stanley glanced around. "Isn't there someplace we could talk more privately?"

"I have to park the van. I suppose you can come along," Lark said reluctantly. She held back a sigh. Nothing was changed. It was all just the way it was before, Stanley being sweet and concerned and understanding, she feeling despicable and guilty because she didn't love him.

She lifted her eyes to his open blue eyes, desperately wishing once again that she could love him. He was basically such a nice person, pleasant-looking, an excellent dentist, a trustworthy friend. She *should* love him, she thought, berating herself. It would make a lot more sense than loving Rand. But she knew she didn't and never would.

She drove the van around to the parking area and turned off the engine. She kept her hands on the wheel, nervously wondering what Stanley was going to say. He reached awkwardly across the bucket seats of the van and touched her hand.

"May I kiss you?" he asked gently.

Lark hesitated, not wanting the kiss and yet not wanting to hurt him either. Just then, over Stanley's shoulder she saw the pickup pull up next to the van. Rand was at the wheel. She saw him eye the van and its occupants curiously.

In that instant a jumble of thoughts suddenly ricocheted through Lark's mind. She remembered Rand's possessive look that night Mr. Desmond made the pass at her. She thought of the jealousy that same action had aroused in him and the passion of his kiss that followed. And Gloria and her friends were talking just today about Rand's possessively jealous nature. . . .

Lark deliberately turned her mouth to Stanley, eyes closed as she swayed toward him. She felt his breath catch in surprise, and then his arms embraced her awkwardly across the bucket seats. It was a pleasant kiss, certainly not repulsive, but hardly earth-shattering. Lark's eyes opened even before it ended, and she saw Rand striding away from the pickup.

For a moment she felt a stab of dismay. He didn't care! She could kiss a dozen men in front of him and he wouldn't blink an eye.

But when he looked back over his shoulder she felt a surge of triumph at the dark anger on his face. If he didn't care, he would have been indifferent, not angry!

Deliberately, as Rand watched, Lark tilted her head and Stanley obligingly kissed her again. She was startled to see a damp sheen of perspiration on his forehead when they finally parted. The kiss had obviously had a great deal more of an effect on Stanley than it had on her. She bit her lip guiltily, realizing that unjustly raising his hopes was not a kind thing to do.

Stanley was obviously shaken. "Lark, I . . . Forgive me. It's just that I've missed you so much. I just lost control."

Lark looked at him, stifling another sigh. He was blaming himself for "losing control" when she knew very well that whatever happened had been her doing.

She tried not to think of Rand's passionate lovemaking and how Stanley's kiss paled by comparison. She opened her mouth to apologize, to tell Stanley what she had done was unforgivable, but he touched a finger to her lips.

"Don't say anything now. We'll have plenty of time to talk. I've already registered at the lodge."

"Registered at the lodge?" Lark echoed in dismay. "But . . . but you can't do that!"

"I've already done it," Stanley answered, looking pleased with himself. What he felt was his success with the kiss seemed to have made him uncharacteristically masterful. He informed Lark that he was taking her into town for dinner that evening.

By that time Benny and the other young guides had come to unload the pickup. Benny yelled over to Lark that Mr. Hammond wanted to talk to her about an error on someone's bill.

Perhaps a quiet dinner away from the lodge would be the best place to get everything straightened out with Stanley, Lark decided reluctantly. She honestly didn't want to hurt him. Why had she ever done such a foolish, irresponsible thing as kissing him like that?

Stanley followed her into the office, and then with a whispered "Seven o'clock?" and a squeeze of her arm, he went on up to the room he had taken. Lark straightened out the matter of the bill, which turned out to be the guest's error, not hers. She was just tidying up her typing desk when Rand paused at the counter. He hadn't yet changed out of the rough clothes he always wore on the river, but there was a self-assured authority about him that transcended clothing. He could have worn rags, Lark thought, and still retained that air of arrogant self-assurance. He handed her a slip of paper with a name and address.

"The Cullisons thought these friends of theirs would be interested in seeing a lodge brochure and price list," he said impersonally.

Lark took the slip of paper. "I'll mail them one immediately."

Rand's expression was set and cold, but there was a hint of reluctant curiosity in his voice when he said, "You appeared to be having a good time out in the van." He raised a dark eyebrow. "Old friend? Or new acquaintance?"

Lark hesitated and then said, "It was Stanley. I decided you were right about my treating him unfairly, so I wrote to him."

"You asked him to come here?" His voice held taut surprise.

"No, that was his own idea."

"I'm sure he must have been gratified to receive such a warm welcome to his surprise visit," Rand said caustically.

Lark looked up at him, her heart thudding with the sure knowledge that Rand was jealous. She shoved into the background of her mind her dread of the moment when she must tell Stanley the truth about that kiss. "You know what they say," she murmured with deliberate carelessness. "Absence makes the heart grow fonder."

Rand disdained an answer to that remark and spun on his heel, his face dark with anger. Lark set the slip of paper by the typewriter, hands trembling. Gloria's friend had said that taunting Rand was like playing with fire, and Lark had the shaky feeling that fire had almost burst into flaming explosion just now. But in spite of her trembling she felt a strange exhilaration in knowing that she had affected Rand that way, that he cared.

Later, she went to the dorm room, showered, and manicured her nails with a frosty polish. She dressed carefully in her most flattering outfit, a pale peach chiffon with fitted waist and draped neckline that showed off her slim figure to perfection. With it she wore white high-heeled sandals that emphasized her shapely legs, and dangling hoop earrings. She seldom wore much makeup, but the outfit seemed to call for something dramatic. She rummaged in Pam's well-equipped cosmetics box until she found mascara and a smoky eye shadow that added just the proper touch of sophisticated mystery.

Pam wandered in for a few minutes' rest before serving dinner. She stopped short when she saw Lark.

"Good Lord, Lark, is that really you?" she gasped. With an expressive roll of her eyes, she added in an exaggerated tone, "I thought I'd stumbled into some movie star's dressing room by mistake!"

Lark twirled in front of her. "Do I look all right?"

"All right!" Pam raised her eyebrows. "Lark, you're going to knock this guy's eyes out. He must be someone really special."

Guiltily Lark realized she had hardly given a thought to Stanley, that the whole effort was for the few moments when she would walk in front of Rand in the living room. But she didn't tell Pam that, of course. Neither did Pam know about that night Lark had spent in Rand's arms. Without actually lying about it, Lark had let Pam and everyone believe she and Rand had spent a sleepless night waiting around the hospital for word of Rand's grandfather's condition.

Stanley was sitting on a sofa near the picture windows when Lark went out. Surreptitiously Lark peered around looking for Rand as Stanley walked toward her, his face lit up as if she had just given him some marvelous gift.

"You look gorgeous," he murmured. His lips brushed her temple. "You remembered that was my favorite dress, didn't you?"

Lark hadn't remembered, of course. She had only wanted to impress Rand, and she was suddenly dismayed by Stanley's possessive grip on her arm and wished she had worn something dull and shapeless. It was all wasted effort anyway. Rand was nowhere around.

But suddenly he was there, standing in the doorway to the dining room. He had changed clothes too, to an expensive, impeccably tailored dark suit and crisp white shirt and stylish tie. He had one hand raised, leaning casually against the door frame, and he eyed Lark with the appraising look of a predator considering his prey. Lark's heart suddenly pounded at the unexpected combination of the savage and sophisticated.

"I don't believe I've met your friend," Rand remarked.

Uneasily Lark made introductions, and the men shook hands. Stanley looked puzzled, as if he sensed undercurrents here that he did not understand. Lark could tell he did not like the way Rand was eyeing her openly, almost brazenly, as if he could see right through the filmy dress. Her only consolation was that she knew she had succeeded in catching Rand's attention and perhaps even arousing his jealousy. She also had the uneasy feeling it might somehow turn out to be a hollow victory.

"You're looking unusually lovely tonight." Rand's remark was coupled with another boldly appraising inspection.

"Thank you," she murmured uneasily. She eyed his dark suit.

"Are you . . . ? I mean . . ."

"Gloria's friends expressed an interest in seeing the town," he said smoothly, "so I'm taking them in after dinner."

"Gloria too?" The words were out before Lark could stop them, and she knew her dismay was all too obvious.

He shrugged and smiled lazily, neither confirming nor denying her suspicion. "So perhaps we'll run into you later."

He turned away, effectively dismissing them, and quite ruining Lark's mental image of herself sweeping grandly by him on Stanley's arm. Was he deliberately going out with Gloria and her friends to get even with *her*? Lark wondered unhappily.

"Who the hell is he?" Stanley muttered, sounding half-angry, half-perplexed. "I don't like the way he looked at you."

"He's just one of the river guides," Lark said, trying to regain her earlier satisfaction with Rand's jealousy. It wouldn't return, and she kept seeing those knowing, mocking eyes.

They ate at a restaurant with an outside deck overlooking the river. The tables were lit with flickering candles, and soft guitar music drifted up from the lounge below. It was an intimate, romantic setting, but Lark kept up a bright chatter about the river and the lodge, mutual acquaintances back in Seattle, and Stanley's dental practice. They ate tender salmon steaks and baked potatoes with sour cream and bits of bacon and chives. It was all delicious and yet Lark hardly tasted anything. Stanley kept getting quieter, his answers to her animated but inconsequential questions more monosyllabic. Finally he covered her hand with his.

"Lark, what's wrong?" he asked earnestly. "I don't know what to think. First you didn't seem glad to see me at all. Then you kissed me like . . . like you'd never kissed me before. Now you act as if you must keep making conversation so I won't have a chance to say something you don't want to hear. And I'm sure you know what it is I want to say if you'll give me half a chance."

Lark was suddenly filled with remorse. Walking out on Stanley the first time was bad enough, but what she had done tonight was even worse. She had tried to use Stanley, just as she suspected Rand had used her in his game of love with Gloria. She toyed uneasily with the fragile glass holding the pale rosé wine Stanley had ordered.

"It has something to do with that guy you introduced at the lodge, doesn't it?" he asked knowingly.

Lark nodded miserably.

"Do you want to tell me about it?"

Slowly, haltingly, Lark related how she had met and fallen in love with Rand and how she had used Stanley today in a deliberate attempt to make Rand jealous. "I'm sorry," she whispered finally. "It was a rotten, unforgivable thing to do. I think so much of you, Stanley, but . . ." Her voice trailed off helplessly.

"I know. You'll always think of me as a good friend. But not as a lover." He smiled a little sadly. "I suppose I've always known that. It's just that I still hoped, I guess."

"You're too nice, Stanley." Lark sighed unhappily. "You should be furious with me instead of understanding."

"Sometimes I wish I could be furious with you, and rant and rave and throw things. But I suppose I'm just the nonviolent type." Stanley sighed, and Lark held back a smile, quite unable to imagine calm, nontemperamental Stanley behaving in such a fashion. He took a sip of the wine and eyed her thoughtfully. "I'm not so sure about your friend Rand, though."

"What do you mean?" Lark asked uneasily.

The waitress came, deftly removing plates and offering dessert. Lark shook her head but requested coffee. Stanley waited until the waitress was gone before he spoke again.

"I'd say, if you were trying to make Rand jealous, that you probably succeeded. He certainly had the look of a jealous man there at the lodge tonight. But you could be playing a very dangerous game."

Lark's heart did an unexpected flip-flop. "You think Rand is . . . dangerous?"

"I don't think he is the kind of man who will ever be described as putty in some woman's hands," Stanley said dryly. He looked down at Lark's hand, no longer adorned by his engagement ring, the healthy skin honey tan against the snowy white tablecloth. "Even hands as lovely as yours." He hesitated. "How does Rand feel about you?"

Lark shrugged dispiritedly. "I don't know. Gloria Hammond, the lodge owner's daughter, is in love with him. She's very attractive. Sometimes I think he's just using me to punish her for something she did in the past."

"If he hurts you . . ." Stanley began warningly, his fists uncharacteristically clenching.

"If he hurts me, it will be exactly what I deserve for being foolish enough to fall in love with him." Lark glanced at the watch on her left wrist. "We'd better be getting back."

Stanley nodded. "I'll be leaving in the morning."

Lark didn't argue, guiltily relieved that he wasn't staying. Stanley helped her into her light spring wrap, and they drove back to the lodge, each absorbed in private thoughts. At the end of the hallway to the employees' quarters, Stanley's lips brushed her cheek in what she knew was a final farewell kiss. His parting smile was suspiciously bright-eyed.

Lark felt miserable. Stanley went upstairs to his room. She walked slowly down the hallway to the dorm but hesitated outside the door. A crack of light showed underneath. It wasn't late, and Pam would be waiting to hear all about the evening. Lark turned away, not wanting to talk to anyone just yet. She tiptoed silently behind a middle-aged couple watching television in the living room and slipped through the doors to the redwood deck.

Outside, she leaned against the railing, listening to the rumble of the river. Moonlight turned the rapids to silver foam and shot a mirror gleam across the calmer stretch of water.

Lark felt a curious mixture of emotions swirling through her as a cool, damp breeze brushed her face. She felt guilty and regretful over what she had done to Stanley, both for her inability to love him and her shameful exploitation of him in trying to make Rand jealous. And yet, in spite of her guilt and regret and shame, she couldn't help a little flicker of triumph that came with knowing Rand *was* jealous. Even Stanley had noticed it.

Suddenly she was aware that she was not alone. There had been no sound, no footsteps, but she whirled, one hand at her slender throat.

"Rand! I . . . I didn't hear you come out."

"Perhaps your thoughts were elsewhere." His voice was mocking. The only light on the deck was the flickering glow from the living-room windows, and his broad-shouldered figure made a menacing silhouette against the light. He turned slightly. His suit jacket was open and he had loosened his tie. He still looked sophisticated, but in a negligent, reckless way. "Am I interrupting anything?" he inquired, looking around pointedly.

"Stanley went to his room."

"That seems a peculiar way to end an . . . intimate evening."

"Much different than the way you end most of your dates, I'm sure," Lark retorted acidly. "By the way, where are Gloria and her friends?"

Rand's well-built shoulders moved in a careless shrug. "Susan and Francie were not particularly impressed with the entertainment our small town had to offer on a weekday evening."

"How disappointing," Lark murmured.

"Your evening also seems to have ended rather early," Rand remarked. "Will Stanley be staying long?"

"He's leaving in the morning."

Rand raised a dark eyebrow. "Lovers' quarrel?"

"Don't be ridiculous," Lark said in a low voice. "I'm not in love with him. I never have been. I told you that." She pulled the evening wrap around her, a gesture that was more protective than warming. She was uneasily aware of Stanley's warning that Rand was not a man to be trifled with, and she had the feeling his calm, collected air masked an explosive force just beneath the surface, a force with which she had recklessly toyed.

Still the calm, thoughtful air remained. "Your claim of indifference toward Stanley hardly seems in keeping with the way you welcomed him in the van."

"I made a mistake," she said tightly. "I apologized to him."

He took a stride toward her, and his hands gripped her

arms like a vise. "You did it deliberately to make me jealous, didn't you?"

Lark lifted anguished eyes to his. "Yes! Yes, I did. It was a terrible, unforgivable thing to do to Stanley."

"But a perfectly acceptable thing to do to me," Rand retorted harshly.

"No, it wasn't. I . . ."

"Then why did you do it?"

Why? Because she was afraid Gloria was right, that he was only using her, as despicably as she had used Stanley. Because she was desperate enough to use any means to arouse his interest. Because she was in love with him.

When she didn't answer immediately, his hands released her disdainfully, almost pushing her away from him. "I'm sure you'll be pleased to know you succeeded," he said, his voice icy with contempt. "From the minute I saw you in the van with him, I've been burning with jealousy. Tonight I didn't know whether it was you or Stanley I wanted to tear apart with my bare hands." He took a deep breath, fighting the raging fury within him. "But then I realized he probably is a pretty decent kind of guy and didn't deserve either what I was thinking about doing to him or what you *were* doing to him."

Lark quaked under the leashed fury and contempt in his voice, knowing he was not finished, that his full condemnation of her was yet to come. In the dim light his features were darkly demoniacal. A whisper of wind raked an oak branch across the shake roof and swirled the filmy chiffon material of her dress around her slim legs. It seemed an aeon ago that she had foolishly chosen to wear it.

"And as for you . . ." he began. His look of scorn and disdain flicked over her skin like a whip. "I decided you weren't worth the trouble."

Lark stared at him, feeling something shrivel inside her. It would have been terrible enough if he had called her the vicious, disrespectful names she had silently been calling herself. But this ruthless dismissal of any possible worth she might lay claim to was even worse.

She swallowed convulsively, her throat tight and dry. The moonlight on the river seemed brittle and glassy now, as if it might splinter into a thousand cutting shards. Lark felt on the edge of splintering too, as if she might shatter in a million dying pieces.

But from somewhere deep inside her character she dredged up the strength to straighten her head and respond. "I admitted I was wrong, and I am sorry for what I did. I was unfair to both you and Stanley. But at least I can admit I was wrong, which I think is more than you are capable of doing."

"I'm afraid I don't understand the point you're trying to make," he said coldly.

"The point I am trying to make is that although I may have provoked your jealousy, it's only your pride that is damaged, not your . . . heart." Lark's voice faltered and she almost choked on the final word, but she swallowed and forced herself to go on. "You've never cared for me except as a useful tool to teach Gloria a lesson and punish her for running off and marrying another man. You knew she was watching when you kissed me. You deliberately kissed me where she couldn't fail to see—"

"You little fool!" he exploded. "Yes, I knew she was probably watching, but I didn't give a damn. I didn't care if the whole world was watching. I kissed you because I wanted to. Because I was falling in love with you!"

Lark stared at him, stunned and speechless. *Falling in love with you.* The words spiraled through her mind. The wind lifted her long, silky hair, furling it around her face, and she brushed at it distractedly. "But Gloria said—"

"I don't give a damn what Gloria said! And neither should you."

"You were in love with her!" Lark cried. "You can't deny that. Everyone knew it!"

"I can and do deny it," Rand said flatly.

"You intended to marry her—"

"Gloria intended to marry me. There is a world of difference."

"I don't understand," Lark said, almost in a whisper. "Mrs. Quigley thought . . . Everyone thought . . ."

"Do you really believe I give a damn what people think?" Rand retorted.

"You were never in love with Gloria?" Lark whispered in tremulous bewilderment.

"My parents and the Hammonds were friends before I was born. When my father was killed, my mother came very near to having a complete breakdown. The Hammonds were wonderful to us. I lived with them for a while when my mother went away to recuperate. I'll always feel indebted to them." He paused, his lip curling slightly. "Unfortunately, Gloria is notably lacking in their warm, generous qualities."

"But not in sex appeal, as I'm sure you've noticed!" Lark flared.

Rand shrugged. "Of course I noticed. What man wouldn't, the way she flaunts it? And I won't deny . . . certain aspects of our relationship in the past. But I was never in love with her, nor did I intend to marry her, in spite of my gratitude and affection for the Hammonds."

The light went out in the living room, leaving them in the brittle moonlight. Wind rustled lightly through the oaks and sighed through the stately cedars. Lark felt bewildered, oddly lost, as if she had stepped off the security of solid ground and into shifting quicksand.

"It doesn't seem likely Gloria would assume you were planning to marry her unless she had some reason to believe it," Lark said faintly.

"I do not pretend to understand the devious workings of a woman's mind," Rand said bluntly. "I do know what Gloria *did*. She tried every trick, every ploy, to induce me to marry her." There was no boasting in his voice, merely statement of fact. "Frankly, I don't know why. She had plenty of other admirers."

But Lark knew why, feeling about him, loving him as she did. Even now, as she wilted under his scorn and anger, the love was still there, like an ache deep within her.

"Finally Gloria tried jealousy. A businessman named David Riegal came up from San Francisco on vacation and stayed at the lodge. He fell in love with Gloria and she deliberately used him to try to make me jealous." He paused, his voice coldly contemptuous. "As you used Stanley."

"I told you I was wrong!" Lark said wildly.

Rand cut curtly into her apology. "Gloria decided to take a gamble."

"What sort of gamble?" Lark's throat felt raw, her voice unable to rise above a whisper.

"She left a note telling me she and David Riegal were eloping to Reno and that if I didn't do something to stop them she was going to go ahead and marry him."

"And what did you do?"

"Nothing," he said flatly. "And so Gloria did what she had threatened and married David Riegal. She let everyone think she had dumped me. Maybe she even believed it herself after a while. As I've said, I don't really give a damn what people think."

In spite of the throbbing ache within her, Lark could feel a moment of pity for Gloria in her desperate gamble. How little Gloria had really known Rand, even after growing up with him, if she thought she could manipulate and control him. And she was still making the same mistake, Lark thought, remembering Gloria's conversation with her friends in the van.

"What happened on the river trip?" Lark asked in a low voice. "With the man from Ohio."

"Gloria tried the same trick again. Is it all you women ever think of?"

"But Gloria thought you were jealous."

"Gloria mistakes disgust for jealousy," he said caustically.

"And so did I," Lark murmured despairingly.

There was a moment of strained silence, and then Rand said harshly, "No, that isn't true. I *was* jealous of you and Stanley. I could hardly think straight when I saw him kissing you." Brutally he added, "He doesn't know how lucky he is that you aren't in love with him. He's a decent guy. He deserves better."

"Oh, yes, you hold yourself up as so superior," Lark said bitterly, finally finding voice again. She tossed her hair back, unconscious of the moonlight highlighting the golden strands. "But you continued your relationship after Gloria was married. Even if you didn't want her, you didn't want David Riegal to have her either. You broke up her marriage just for ... for spite."

"The trips to San Francisco?" he questioned mockingly. "Oh, I heard the rumors. What the gossipers never bothered to find out was what I did on those trips to California, or why I went. One reason was business, plain and simple. The other was the fact that my mother lives just outside San Francisco."

Lark caught her breath, momentarily angry at Mrs. Quigley for filling her full of such erroneous gossip, then angry at herself for ever having believed it. Then she had to sigh inwardly. Whatever Mrs. Quigley told her had been said without malicious or harmful intent; she was only concerned for Lark and trying to keep her from being hurt.

"And you never even saw Gloria on any of those trips?" Lark asked tremulously.

Rand hesitated. He paced along the deck, wind ruffling his crisp hair. Moonlight hollowed his chiseled cheekbones. "I did see her once. She called me with some wild tale about how David was mistreating her and how she desperately needed someone to help her. So I went down there. I felt, for her parents' sake, I owed her that much."

"This is when her marriage broke up?"

"This is when I told her David was better than she deserved, and if she had any sense she'd stop acting like a spoiled brat and try to be a good wife to him," he said.

"But . . . but if you didn't cause her marriage to break up, what did?" Lark asked, bewildered. Everything was so different from what she had believed all along. She couldn't seem to think straight.

Rand shrugged. "I'm sure I don't know. Perhaps David finally recognized what a deceptive, manipulative . . ." He broke off, and Lark knew he was on the verge of using a vulgarly descriptive word. ". . . woman she really is," he finally finished abruptly. His lip curled as he looked down at Lark again. "Unfortunately, being devious and manipulative is something you seem to share with Gloria."

Suddenly he paused in his restless pacing and stopped directly in front of her. He was only inches away, his face harsh and cold in the moonlight, his anger and contempt overpowering. He reached out and pulled her to him roughly, callously ignoring her gasp of pain as his fingers bit cruelly into her arms. She felt a flicker of fear and tried to pull away.

"Rand, please, I . . ."

His fingers tightened, then one arm slid around her waist to bend her body to his, arching her back almost painfully and molding her soft curves to the harsh angularity of rock-hard muscles stretched over a skeleton of steel.

"And your manipulating little scheme worked," he muttered, his voice hoarse, damning her even as he told her she had succeeded.

His mouth came down on hers, hard, brutal, bruising. His lips ravished hers, relentless and demanding, and his hand slid inside the draped neckline of her dress and roughly found her breast. The embrace was fiery and yet strangely without warmth, like brilliant northern lights flaming in a distant night sky. She struggled against him, stunned by his anger and brutal condemnation of what she had done, shocked by the fire-and-ice caresses that lacked any sense of tenderness.

And yet in spite of their cold harshness, she found herself responding to his kisses and caresses, found her body aching for remembered ecstasy.

No! She didn't want to respond, wouldn't respond, not when his passion flared in anger instead of love!

But he'd said he was falling in love with her that night he kissed her by the river . . . he'd made love to her as if he loved her. . . . She couldn't let her terrible mistake come between them and ruin everything! She would make him feel again the way he had felt about her the night he made love to her with such sweet, tender passion.

Recklessly she twined her arms around his neck and returned his cold-blooded kisses with blazing passion. She met the brutal probe of his tongue with a fiery, provocative dart of her own, and they collided in silent, intimate duel. She felt him stiffen and pull back in surprise, but she only held him more fiercely.

She stood on tiptoe, holding her mouth to his. She knew she was throwing herself at him, but she didn't care. She must show him what a horrible mistake she had made. She must make him want her as he had once wanted her! She moved her lips against his, caught his lower lip in the delicate trap of her teeth.

He lifted his head, his muscular strength greater than hers, and his mouth was out of her reach. His hands remained rigidly clenched at his sides as she kissed the moon-sculptured angle of his jaw and the throbbing pulse point in his throat. She molded her body against his with shameless abandon, recklessly thrust her breasts against the hard muscles of his chest. And in spite of his rigidly unyielding stance, she felt the unmistakable signal of male arousal beginning against her straining body.

"We could go somewhere. Your house . . ." She tilted her head back, trying to tempt him with the mouth that he had once said he found irresistible. "Your room . . . anywhere!" she ended on an almost pleading note as he made no move to take her offered mouth.

With a snarled oath he suddenly reached up and untangled her hands from behind his neck. "What the hell are you trying to do?" he demanded harshly. "Why are you acting as if you want me to take you right here on the deck?"

She stared up at him, lips parted. Yes, her brazen behavior was a deliberate attempt to arouse his passion. But it was no act. She *loved* him! She wanted him, wanted him right now in the most earthy and basic way possible. But she wanted him for tomorrow too, tomorrow and always.

"I . . ." She wanted to say: *I love you*! And yet she couldn't. She could throw herself at him in wanton abandon, but she couldn't say the words that bared her soul to his merciless gaze. "I want to stay all night with you." She reached for his hand and deliberately placed it on the rounded curve of her breast. "I want to make love with you . . . again."

He looked down at her, his chiseled mouth thinned to a hard slash across his face. She felt the small, almost imperceptible movements of his fingertips around the tip of her breast, almost as if they moved against his will. Their eyes held in locked conflict as they both felt the taut hardening under the manipulation of his fingertips. A muscle jerked along his jawline as if the response angered him.

Bravely her arms stole around his neck again. As if challenging the validity of her offer, his hands roamed her body without restraint, as if he intended placing his fingerprints on every inch of her. One hand boldly slid beneath the frothy chiffon to caress the slim line of her thigh and the rounded curve of her hips, the thin sheen of panty hose the only barrier between roughly invading hand and silken skin. He held her to him in a way that left no doubt about his fully aroused male passion, and yet the dark twist of anger on his face denied everything his body and marauding hands proclaimed.

"Does it hurt you to admit you want me?" she challenged. She felt strangely near some breaking point, hovering on the knife edge of a plunge into an unknown chasm.

"Does it please you to know you're driving me wild?" he retorted. With a raw sound that was half-groan, half-growl, his hands left their prowling exploration and his arms wound around her in hungry embrace. No longer were his kisses deliberately, coldly calculated. A molten flame engulfed them, and they swirled at the center of a firestorm, caught in a primitive desire heightened by memories of that other night, swept along by the intoxicating knowledge that the ecstasy could happen again.

At that moment Lark lost all sense of deliberate intent, of what she had been trying to do to him. She was in his power, body and soul. She loved him.

Then, with a muttered oath and a self-control dredged from the depths of some steel core of his character, he thrust her away from him and turned on his heel. She clutched the railing for balance, dizzied by the suddenness of his brutal rejection.

"Rand!" she cried.

"Congratulations," he muttered thickly.

She slumped against the rail as his figure disappeared around the corner of the lodge. *Congratulations.* The bitter word said it all. She had succeeded. She had aroused his jealousy. She had ignited the incandescent blaze of his passion.

But it was indeed a hollow victory, because his fragile awakening love for her had died.

Chapter Nine

Lark roused sluggishly from a restless sleep. Her head throbbed and her eyes felt swollen. Her heart was pounding and she had the vague, unpleasant feeling that she hadn't slept at all, that all night she had been running, fleeing wildly to escape some awful, nameless terror that was bearing down on her.

For a moment her numbed mind refused to separate dream from reality and to dredge up what had really happened. She was aware only of the sick feeling that something terrible *had* happened.

Then, with the stabbing pain of a knife plunged into her heart, it all came back to her. Rand's cold contempt and fury, the startling revelation of his real relationship with Gloria, the bruising, brutal embrace and kiss. And then the devastating knowledge that he had been falling in love with her but now she had lost him forever.

Dully, seeking to ease the pain that was an almost physical ache, she rolled over in bed, vaguely wondering what had roused her at such an early hour. Gray dawn was just beginning to light the room's single window. Then she heard again what must have wakened her, the sound of a car engine.

She raised up on one elbow and pushed the curtain aside to peer outside. Stanley was loading luggage into the trunk of his car while the engine warmed up. She ought to hurry and dress and go out and tell him goodbye, she thought guiltily. But her sluggish body made no effort to carry out the thought, and a moment later she abandoned it. Stanley was obviously leaving at such an early hour to avoid some painful, awkward good-bye scene with her. There was no need to make things more difficult for him. She had done enough to hurt him already.

She slumped down again, remembering how she had wandered aimlessly for what must have been hours last night after Rand scornfully thrust her aside and stalked away. She hadn't come inside until the moon sank behind the mountains and her hair and clothes were damp from the night dew.

The chiffon dress was ruined, she thought dully, eyeing the crumpled peach-colored froth on the floor, the material ripped and torn from her mindless wanderings around the grounds. It didn't seem of any importance. Pam had been asleep when she finally crept in, so she was spared talking about what had happened. She had no memory of crying, only of staring open-eyed into the darkness once she was in bed, but her swollen, aching eyes gave evidence that tears had not been lacking.

Rand had been in love with her, if only for a brief time. The thought held a kind of wild, sweet agony, an exquisite pain. She thought of that first kiss in the moonlight, wild, passionate, even bruising. She trembled to the memory of the sweet fire of their lovemaking. And it had all ended in last night's coldly brutal embrace.

Perhaps it would have been better if she had never known of his love, she thought, turning her face to the wall. Perhaps the pain would be more bearable if she wasn't left with the agonizing dreams of what might have been. She had been foolish and proud, resorting to immature game playing. She could hardly blame Rand for putting her in the same class with shallow, scheming Gloria. And so now she had lost him forever.

For a moment a flicker of resentment rose within her. It was partly because of Rand that she had written to Stanley in the first place, responding to his accusations about her "running away." Rand shouldn't blame her because Stanley showed up wanting to revive their relationship.

But the flicker of resentment died in guilt. She, and she alone, had made the shallow, selfish decision to use Stanley so heartlessly. She, and she alone, had tried to manipulate and control Rand by arousing his jealousy. If her heart were not breaking, she could almost laugh at her foolishness in ever thinking she could manipulate a man such as Rand. For that was what she had tried to do, of course, as surely as Gloria had tried the same trick.

She dozed again, finally waking only when Pam shook her shoulder. Lark murmured something about skipping breakfast this morning. Pam, misunderstanding, just laughed and made a teasing comment about her late date with Stanley.

Lark went directly to her office desk when she finally managed to get out of bed. She saw Rand several times. He made no effort to avoid her. He had business to conduct running the timber company and spent a good hour on the office telephone, oblivious of her existence.

Lark was relieved when Rand left later that same day on another river run. She was probably the only one who was *not* surprised when Gloria abruptly left for San Francisco without mention of returning. Lark knew now that Rand was finished with Gloria, and Gloria had finally realized it, but there was no satisfaction in the thought. Perhaps she could even have consoled herself more easily if he had turned to Gloria. Then she could shift the blame to Gloria, blame her own loss on the other girl's seductive ways and lush beauty and cleverness. As it was, she had to live with the knowledge that she had defeated herself with her devious attempt at manipulation. No one else had won; she had simply lost.

Lark kept her aching heart to herself, going about her duties competently but lifelessly. Over and over she searched her mind for something she could say to Rand, something that would rekindle the flame of love that had died. Her own love hadn't died. Sometimes she wished desperately that it would, but she had the hopeless feeling that it would always be there, an eternal, torturing ache.

She drove the van downriver, as usual, to pick up the guests at the end of the river trip. The van might have been driven by a robot for all the attention Rand gave her. And Lark *felt* like a robot, doing the job mechanically, only wishing she had a switch to turn off her aching emotions and regret.

Rand was on the phone again as soon as he got back to the lodge, giving instructions about a government timber bid, authorizing purchase of some plywood-mill equipment, talking to one of the state's senators in Washington, D.C., about some pending timber legislation. He couldn't continue running the company from a distance much longer, Lark thought. The business was too big, too complex, the strain of double responsibility too much. And yet when Rand asked Mr. Hammond if anyone had been found to take his place as head guide yet, and no one had, he gave no hint of abandoning his guiding responsibilities at the lodge.

That situation changed abruptly the following morning. Rand had evidently taken the task of finding his replacement into his own hands, and he turned up a man named Hank Anderson. Anderson had once run a fishing-guide service on the Rogue but had been mining in Alaska for the past few years.

The conference among Rand, Mr. Hammond, and Hank Anderson took place around the counter that separated Lark's office from the main lobby, and everything was settled within a few minutes. Hank was hired and would start guiding for the lodge immediately, and Rand would be leaving just as immediately.

That outcome wasn't unexpected, of course. It was what Rand had been waiting for. And for Rand's sake, Lark could be glad it happened now, to take the strain of double responsibility off his shoulders. But for herself . . .

Concealing a stray tear that threatened to spill down her cheek, Lark slipped past the men to take the morning's output of letters to the mailbox for the rural mail carrier.

Her pace slowed as soon as she was away from the building. Rand was leaving the lodge. After today, she would probably never see him again. Seeing him, feeling his contemptuous indifference toward her, was painful enough, but the prospect of not seeing him at all was infinitely worse.

Her steps dragged as she approached the big wooden mailbox. All the energy and life seemed drained from her. Almost absentmindedly she realized the mail carrier's car was approaching. With an automatic smile she handed him the outgoing letters and he handed her a bundle of mail directly instead of putting it in the box.

If the letter addressed to her hadn't been on top of the bundle, Lark probably wouldn't even have noticed it, so lost was she in her own unhappy thoughts. It was from the lawyer in Seattle. Without particular interest she tore the envelope open. To her astonishment a check fell into her hands. A check for just over two thousand dollars!

She read the letter of explanation with equal astonishment. The forms and papers she had signed and sent to the lawyer earlier had enabled him to complete everything, and the enclosed check was the final settlement of her father's estate. He sounded slightly apologetic that there was not more, but to Lark, who had never expected to receive anything, it seemed like a small fortune. The lawyer made no mention of Stanley this time.

Lark was still studying the check in astonishment as she approached the office door. Rand was just coming out. They looked at each other, and as always, the sight of him started a trembling in her body that spread from the heart of her desire. Some comment seemed called for, if only to keep Rand from realizing how his presence affected her.

"Hank Anderson appears very capable. I'm sure Mr. Hammond is relieved that you were able to find someone so experienced to take your place."

"Yes, I'm sure Hank will do fine."

"How is your grandfather now?"

"He'll be going home from the hospital in a few days. He'll have a full-time nurse for a while, and my mother is also coming up for a few weeks to make sure he minds the nurse's orders."

It was a stilted, meaningless conversation, as impersonal as if they were strangers instead of two people who had shared one unforgettable night of love. Or perhaps, Lark thought with an inward wrench of pain, it was only she who had found that night unforgettable.

Eyes averted to hide a giveaway glitter of tears, she brushed on by him with some hastily muttered excuse about work. When she peered out the office window a few moments later, he was gone, as gone as if he had stepped into another world. And left hers forever.

Lark floundered through the day. The future stretched out bleak and empty before her, and she seemed to be battered by reminders of Rand from all sides. The photographs on the office wall, everyday references by the other guides to something Rand had said or done, a new female guest asking plaintively, "You mean that good-looking Rand Whitcomb I've heard so much about isn't here anymore?" She found herself staring at the spot on the deck where Rand had kissed her with such cold harshness. She felt drawn to the rocky point where his first kiss had awakened the unfamiliar hungers of passion within her.

It was two days before the realization struck her that she didn't have to stay here where she could not escape reminders of the love she had lost. The internal memories would always be there, of course. They would always be a part of her. But she could escape the external reminders that endlessly bombarded her. It was a lack of funds that had trapped her here originally, but with the check from the lawyer she was no longer in that financial predicament. She could give her notice to the Hammonds and be on her way to a new life in San Diego. There was nothing to hold her here now.

She could almost hear Rand contemptuously telling her that she was running away again, but she determinedly closed her mind to such thoughts. Mr. Hammond came into the office just a few minutes later and Lark quickly made her decision official. She hadn't taken the time to give any thought to what Mr. Hammond's reaction would be. She was thinking only of her own desperate need to get away, and she was unprepared for the sudden frown on Mr. Hammond's usually cheerful face.

"This will be very inconvenient for us. It's hard to break in someone new when the season is in full swing as it is now. We expected you to stay the full season."

"I'm sure someone competent can be found." Lark felt dismayed by his unhappy expression, and a sudden surge of guilt assailed her. In her agitation and distress she had forgotten all about her earlier agreement to stay with the job all season. They really had no way to hold her to that, of course, but it wasn't fair to leave them in midseason. "I'm really sorry. Something . . . unexpected has come up. I'll stay on until someone can be found to replace me, of course," she added, hoping that would help to ease the situation.

"First Rand says he's leaving. Then my daughter picks up and heads back to San Francisco. Now you're leaving." Mr. Hammond's expression was suddenly thoughtful. "Is there some connection?"

Lark struggled to keep her voice casual. "Just coincidence, I suppose," she murmured evasively.

"Well, if you feel you have to leave, I suppose you have to."

Mr. Hammond still didn't sound very happy, and Lark was almost afraid to bring up the other subject that was on her mind. Then she took a deep breath and plunged ahead.

"Would it be possible, sometime before I leave, for me to go along on a trip down the river? I'd pay my way, of course, the same as any other guest. I've wanted to go ever since I first heard about the white-water trips."

"We always allow each employee one free trip down the river each season," Mr. Hammond said.

"I'm hardly entitled to that, since I'm leaving long before the end of the season."

"I think it's a good idea for you to go," Mr. Hammond said unexpectedly. He gave her a thoughtful look. "You haven't been acting like yourself lately. Maybe a run down the river will change your outlook on whatever is bothering you."

Lark was dismayed to realize her drooping spirits had been so obvious, but at least Mr. Hammond did not seem to know the cause. Lark suspected Pam did know, but so far Lark had evaded Pam's tentative attempts to talk about it with her.

Mr. Hammond checked the guest lists for the next several river trips, but all were booked full. Finally he suggested Lark pick whichever trip she wanted and simply ride on the raft that carried supplies and gear. It would be less comfortable than the passenger rafts, but safe enough. Mrs. Hammond could handle Lark's usual task of driving the van down to transport everyone back.

Lark swiftly decided to go along on the next trip, scheduled for three days later. By the time she returned, perhaps Mr. Hammond would have found someone to replace her, and she could spend a few days training the new girl.

Lark looked forward to the trip with anticipation, and resolutely tried to keep her mind off Rand, though she

was seldom completely successful at that. Thoughts of
him were always there, hovering just below the surface,
no matter what her conscious mind was doing, always
ready to stab her with regret.

Mrs. Quigley and Pam were sorry to hear Lark was
leaving. Mrs. Quigley, with a significant look at Pam,
said it was a shame to lose such a diligent worker. The
irrepressible Pam did one of her best imitations behind
Mrs. Quigley's back, expertly parodying Mrs. Quigley's
scowl. Lark knew Pam could tell she was depressed and
was trying to cheer her up. Pam tried later to talk Lark
into staying, reminding her how much more pleasant it
would be now, with Gloria gone. Pam tentatively
brought up the subject of Rand, but Lark quickly turned
the conversation to her coming trip down the river and
Pam seemed to accept her decision.

Lark was especially busy the day before the trip was
to start. There was the usual flurry of getting guests registered, plus a trip to the Medford airport to pick up a
middle-aged couple arriving by plane. Lark was glad for
all the activity. It helped keep her mind occupied.

The guides usually held a brief meeting with the
people making the river trip the evening before departure. Lark had already heard everything they had to say,
of course, and did not attend. She knew about wearing
life jackets, staying seated and hanging on in dangerous
places, watching out for rattlesnakes and poison oak.

She did go out and pick up one of the oblong metal
boxes handed out to guests for use in carrying miscel-
laneous items needed during the day. The boxes were actually old army-surplus ammunition cans, waterproof,
and a convenient size for carrying such items as suntan
lotion and small cameras. All other belongings were
packed away under waterproof tarps and were unavail-
able during the day. Lark tucked the necessary suntan
lotion, plus lipstick, sunglasses, a scarf, her little camera,
and some extra film in the ammo box for her own use.

On the morning of departure Lark woke with the dull

ache that seemed to have become an integral part of her being, the ache of knowledge that Rand was gone forever. But at least she didn't literally have to force herself to get out of bed this morning, and she found her spirits lifting a little as she dressed, in anticipation of the trip. She dressed in what experience had taught river-runners was the most practical way to challenge the unpredictable river, in layers. First she slipped into her swimsuit, then comfortable old jeans and a blouse, a heavy sweatshirt for warmth against the morning coolness, and finally a floppy hat for protection from the sun. On her feet she wore canvas shoes, but no socks, because she already knew her feet were going to get wet. In her duffel bag she packed changes of clothing and underthings, extra shoes, a waterproof jacket in case of rain, pajamas, and toiletry items.

After breakfast she carried her ammo can and duffel bag, plus the sleeping bag and air mattress borrowed from the lodge, out to the area where guests were already milling around in anticipation. She went back inside to make sure all the office work was as caught up and organized as possible. It wasn't until she heard the loaded pickup head for the river that she hurried down the trail herself.

It was a glorious day for the trip, she thought, sniffing the morning air, fresh with the fragrance of the river and pines. A raucous blue jay scolded her for reasons known only to himself. The dull roar of the rapids held new meaning for her, since she would soon be riding those turbulent waters. A pleasurable shiver of excitement suddenly shot through her. This was just what she needed, she thought. Fun, excitement, any kind of diversion to make her forget Rand.

The rafts were already in the water when she arrived. Benny and another young guide were loading boxes into the supply raft. Another man, naked to the waist, his bronzed back to Lark, was positioning the boxes for proper weight distribution. He looked familiar, suddenly almost painfully familiar, and when he turned around, his mocking eyes met Lark's.

"Rand!" she gasped.

Rand stepped out of the inflated raft as Lark approached. Conflicting emotions charged through her as she faced his bronzed, pagan figure. She struggled to keep her face and voice composed.

"I . . . I had no idea you would be guiding this trip," she finally managed to say. "I thought Hank Anderson . . ."

"Hank had left his small house trailer up in Portland. I told him I'd fill in for him while he went up to get it." He raised a taunting eyebrow. "You sound as if you might not have come if you had known I was guiding this trip."

Lark couldn't answer that. She was still too stunned. She had thought, *hoped*, the excitement of the trip would take her mind off Rand, and now she must endure the bewildering mixture of pain and pleasure which being in daily close contact with him caused.

"Why *are* you along?" he suddenly asked pointedly.

"Because . . ." She broke off. She wouldn't tell him she was leaving, wouldn't let him know that without him there was nothing for her here, that she was running away. "Because the Hammonds let each lodge employee make a river trip sometime during the season."

They looked at each other, her blue eyes defying him to challenge that statement, his dark eyes mockingly skeptical. Behind him the activity of loading the rafts continued, but Lark was aware only of Rand. He was in his element here on the river. The powerful muscles of his naked chest matched the raw, wild power of the river, and something of the river's ruthlessness glittered in his eyes. And yet she knew that he was no unsophisticated savage, that he was just as much at home in the complex, powerful world of business or in the privacy of a moonlit bedroom.

Lark took a tremulous breath. "Perhaps you wouldn't

have been so generously helpful to Hank if you had known I'd be along on this trip," she said.

"Why would that make any difference to me?" The question came out lazily challenging.

Why indeed? Lark echoed to herself. He didn't care one way or the other if she was along. In fact, his remote expression indicated it was presumptuous of her to think that any action she took might be of interest to him.

His indifference stung her, and she snapped, "Are you sure the company can get along without you for a few days? I seem to recall that you proved you were indispensable."

"One of the abilities of a good manager is knowing when and where to delegate authority," he said calmly.

Lark flushed, put in her place. She was again made bluntly aware that Rand was not just a river guide and caretaker. He was the head of a large and important company. She wondered if any of the guests realized that. Not that he needed anything more to impress the female guests, she thought wryly. Most of them seemed hardly able to take their eyes off his bronzed body as it was.

One of the young guides yelled for a knife to cut a knot that wouldn't come untied. Rand dug in his Levi's and brought out a pocketknife and went to help, dismissing Lark with a curt nod of his head. Lark stepped back, staying a little apart from the others. Watching Rand, she asked herself the same question he had raised. Would she have come along on this trip if she had known Rand would be guiding?

It was a question she found herself unable to answer. Seeing him again, knowing she would see him constantly for the next few days, was like reopening a painful wound. A wound that had not yet begun to heal, perhaps would never heal, but a wound that had settled into a dull ache. Now it was a stabbing pain again as she watched Rand move authoritatively among the rafts, heard him laugh in response to something one of the young women said, and felt his indifference toward her.

And yet another part of her felt joyful in spite of the pain, glad just to be near him.

The rafts were ready now, one guide and four passengers per raft, everyone loaded and eager. The four young secretaries from Los Angeles had immediately latched on to Rand's raft. Lark climbed into the supply raft. She had no padded bench seat like the paying customers, but she found a not-too-uncomfortable niche in the tarpaulin-covered supplies and settled into it. Benny was handling the supply raft this trip. He had his long oars poised and ready, a spare oar resting within easy reach. Rand strode along the shore, pausing when he came to Lark. He looked at her disapprovingly.

"This is where Mr. Hammond told me to ride," she said defensively. "The passenger rafts were booked full."

A quick glance along the lineup of rafts showed the truth of that statement. Rand scowled. "You're sitting farther forward than the other passengers. You're going to get wet," he warned.

"I won't melt."

"Really?" His mouth twitched in a small, knowing smile, and Lark gasped as she realized he was remembering another time, another place, when she had willingly melted in his arms.

"I'll take good care of her, Rand," Benny promised, breaking the taut spell. With a glance at Lark he added teasingly, "I won't dump her out more than three or four times."

"I'll try not to ruin your perfect accident-free record," Lark added tartly to Rand.

Rand did not seem amused. He scowled as if he wondered whether Lark's words held some hidden double meaning.

He was still scowling as he gave orders to shove off, his own raft leading the way. The supply raft brought up the rear. Benny rowed through the still water until the current caught and carried them. He, like the other guides, faced forward to row. Lark remembered Rand once saying grimly that it was best never to turn your back on the unpredictable Rogue, and the words seemed to have extra meaning now.

But along here the Rogue played the genteel lady and the rafts drifted along noiselessly, the ripples of the water a purr more than a roar. This area of the river was open to motorized craft, but they saw none. The birds and wildlife scarcely seemed to notice their passage as they slipped silently by, the only sound the occasional dipping of the oars. Benny pointed out a row of turtles sunning on a half-submerged log, a doe and dappled fawn drinking from a bubbling side stream, a flock of odd, rather hairy-headed ducks he called mergansers.

They passed through a minor rapids, bringing squeals echoing back from the girls in Rand's raft. A few drops of spray hit Lark, but she was mostly conscious of the odd feel of the pliable bottom of the raft beneath her feet. The smooth material rippled and undulated with the river's movement, as if she rode a large, muscled animal rather than an inanimate object.

At one point the rafts pulled over to the bank while Rand and Benny went up to the government ranger station to show their river permits and make sure everything was in order. The day was already warming, and Lark peeled off her sweatshirt. There were more rapids, a couple of them rough enough to bring gasps from Lark, but Benny assured her they were nothing compared to what they would encounter later on.

They drifted past the scarred, stained remains of an old mine. Once it had no doubt been ugly, but time had muted and mellowed the stains, softening them like the blending of an artist's paintbrush.

They stopped on a sandy, secluded beach for lunch. The guides set out sliced ham and cheeses for sandwiches, plus a bowl of Mrs. Quigley's tasty macaroni salad, and melon and cookies for dessert. Then they were on their way again.

As the rafts approached a concrete bridge spanning the river, Lark saw passengers in the rafts ahead putting on life jackets, and Benny told her she'd better slip into one too. She realized now how important it was that the guides know the river thoroughly, since there was little to indicate danger approaching.

Benny pointed out a boat landing just beyond the bridge. He said many of the guided trips started at this point, which was the actual boundary of the Wild Rivers section of the Rogue. Beyond this point no public roads touched the river for miles. Access was by boat or foot only.

"There's no turning back now!" Benny whooped as they swept beyond the boat landing.

Chapter Ten

Lark felt a shiver of excitement and a change in Benny too. Gone was his rather casual, relaxed attitude. He took a firmer grip on the oars. Lark wondered what was ahead.

Then she found out. Rand's raft hit the rapids first, the girls squealing. Lark forgot to watch what was happening to them as their own raft tossed and bucked through the jarring white water. The front of the raft plummeted downward and a spray of water slapped Lark in the face. But before she had time to wipe her eyes, the raft arced upward, leaving her stomach somewhere behind. Lark clutched a rope and shook the spray from her face as they came through on the other side. She was drenched and shaken up inside but strangely exhilarated. Abruptly the water changed to a smooth stretch of glassy green.

But the smoothness was deceptive, she realized as the raft suddenly nosed downward into an abyss with a giant standing wave waiting to engulf them on the other side. The mountain of water broke over the raft, drenching Lark from head to toe in a deluge that made her earlier wetting seem insignificant.

"Sorry!" Benny called cheerfully. "That's not the way

you're supposed to hit that one. Maybe that's why I'm not head guide yet!"

Lark gasped, sputtered, and wiped her face. Water swirled around her feet. Benny tossed her a bucket.

"Bail!" he instructed, still cheerful.

Lark almost panicked, thinking surely the raft was leaking and about to go down. But there were no leaks. The standing wave they had hit had simply spilled what seemed an incredible amount of water into the raft. No wonder everything was so carefully packed to keep it waterproof!

They drifted on. Benny pointed out a mark high above the present river-water surface, saying that point marked the level the river had reached during a flood a few years back. It was hard to believe, but he went on to relate other stories of bridges washed out and swept downstream. Then Lark became aware of a roar in the background, a hostile thunder that made the rapids near the lodge sound like little more than a tinkle. She turned and looked at Benny apprehensively.

He laughed. "Don't worry. That one is too big to navigate. At least for most of us. But Rand has been over it," he added, his voice enviously admiring. "Maybe someday I will too."

The passengers were let out on the left side of the river to walk around thundering Rainie Falls. The rafts, with only the guides in them, went through narrow passages on the far side of the falls. Lark's heart almost stopped as she watched Rand come through the steeper passage, the raft catching on the rocks and hanging there suspended for a moment until he shoved it free and plunged on. It was hard to believe he had once come directly over the falls. The drop wasn't far, but the water fell like an avalanche, thundered into a seething fury of white water that looked as if it could smash anything caught in its churning caldron.

But in another abrupt change of mood, the river just a little farther on was almost as calm and peaceful as a

lake. Several people got out and swam alongside the
rafts. Lark stripped down to her swimsuit and applied
suntan lotion but stayed in the raft. She wasn't much of
a swimmer, and she had a healthy distrust of the river
that fully lived up to its treacherous name.

She relaxed, enjoying the sun as it beat down into the
deep canyon. The slopes were covered with trees,
though sometimes Lark wondered how they clung to the
steep, rocky surfaces. Benny pointed out oak and chin-
quapin, shiny-leaved madrona with smooth russet bark,
willows drooping close to the water, and majestic firs
climbing far up the north-facing slopes. A long-necked
blue heron floated overhead, its hoarse cry at odds with
its graceful appearance.

Then the calm waters ended and life jackets went
back on. Benny shouted out the names as they plunged
through the raging white water. Tyee Rapids, Wildcat
Rapids . . . The names blurred together and all Lark
remembered were the boiling rapids themselves, falling
staircases of white water, swirling whirlpools, chutes of
roaring water, once a rushing channel so close to shore
she had to duck to miss the willows. She bailed water
when necessary, heard a scream once and realized it was
her own voice as they hit a series of standing waves
created by underwater obstacles.

Lark learned why the guides carried an extra oar, too.
The river tore one of Benny's oars right out of his grasp.
Lark watched in horrified astonishment as a whirlpool
sucked it under as it stood straight up in the water. They
recovered the oar, scarred and raw, a little later on. Tremulously Lark realized the river could just as easily suck
an unwary person under the same way, and with far
more disastrous results.

Rand was always in the lead, selecting the proper
route through the dangerous waters. Lark was aware of
how disastrous a wrong choice could be, a fact emphasized when they saw a smaller raft, not in their party,
flip over ahead of them. Fortunately the passengers were

wearing life jackets and recaptured their raft safely, but most of their supplies floated merrily downstream.

She was glad when the supply raft rounded a bend and she saw the other rafts pulled in on a sandy bar to make camp for the night. She had done no real work all day, except the occasional bailing, but her muscles felt taut and weary with tension. A tension that wasn't only from the excitement of running the river, she realized as she watched Rand expertly supervise the unloading of gear and setting up of camp. Because in spite of the thrills and excitement, thoughts of Rand had never been far from her mind all day.

Deliberately she turned away, joining other guests in exploring the river's shoreline. Smooth brown salamanders slithered around in shallow backwater, and a big fish arced into the air after a bug. She climbed over huge jumbled boulders and jumped as a snake glided away. She spread her sleeping bag on the sand and used a pump from the raft to inflate the air mattress.

As preparation of the meal got under way, Lark felt, as an employee rather than a guest, that she should help, but Rand curtly motioned her out of the way. Each guide had a specific job to do and handled it efficiently. Benny's specialty was cooking in the Dutch oven. Lark watched with interest as he mixed up a blueberry cobbler and put it in the heavy cast-iron Dutch oven. He set the oven on coals from the fire, then placed coals on the lid as well. The results, Lark learned a little later, were as delicious as anything baked in the finest kitchen.

Before the cobbler dessert came Rand's expertly broiled steaks plus hash-browned potatoes and crisp salad. Afterward Lark helped with dishes, warily keeping as far away from Rand as possible. One of the guides carefully gathered up litter from the meal and packed it away to be taken out for disposal and not left to mar the wilderness area. As darkness fell, Benny built up the campfire and everyone gathered around to talk and sing and laugh.

It was a bittersweet time for Lark, so close to Rand and yet so far away. The light from the campfire flickered on his tanned face, giving him a reckless, daredevil look. And yet he had today proved his sure expertise on the river, his authority around camp, and there was an air of secure, protective capability about him. It was a devastatingly irresistible combination, and the way the secretaries from Los Angeles clustered around him made it obvious. Lark stayed in the background, away from the fire, but she couldn't blame the girls for the way they acted. She slipped off to bed unnoticed while the others were still discussing the day's events and what was yet to come.

She woke in the morning to the tantalizing aroma of coffee perking over an open wood fire. She wanted to jump up and enjoy a cup immediately, but only Rand was up and moving around. She forced herself to lie in the sleeping bag until the other girls woke. Undressing had been easy under cover of darkness, but in daylight there was much struggling and giggling as the girls awkwardly dressed inside the sleeping bags. After a big breakfast of French toast and succulent ham, the rafts were on the river again.

They hurtled through Russian Rapids with its long series of drops and holes and standing waves, then on to more chutes and rapids interspersed with calmer areas. Slim Pickens Rapids, Black Bar Falls, the majestic sweep of Horseshoe Bend. Once the rear of the raft slammed into a rock wall, jarring Lark out of her protective niche, and Benny gave her a guilty grin. Her feet were always wet from the water swirling around the floor of the raft, and she was often spray-drenched as well, although under the hot beat of the sun, the drenching was not always unwelcome.

The scenery was magnificent, ranging from the breathtaking beauty of the river itself, with its calm green stretches between roaring white-water rapids, to the incredible house-sized boulders and the strange holes carved into solid rock by the action of the river swirling smaller rocks round and round almost like a drill. At Winkle Bar they tied up the rafts and walked up to the old log cabin once owned by the famous western writer Zane Grey, who had used it as a fishing camp. It was well maintained by the current owners, but mellow with age, and Lark thought dreamily of what a marvelous retreat it must have been for the prolific writer. Trying not to be conspicuous about it, Lark avoided Rand as much as possible.

Below Winkle Bar they drifted on calm green waters and Lark tentatively suggested something she had been thinking about. "How about showing me how to handle the oars?" she asked Benny.

"Sure. Nothing to it in water like this."

Lark clambered over the lumpy bulk of the supplies stashed beneath the tarpaulin, and Benny showed her how to hold the oars. They seemed awkwardly long at first, but soon she got the hang of it. She didn't try to make the raft go much faster than the current, just used the oars enough to keep the craft headed downstream and away from the rocky banks.

"I think I'll just take it easy for a little while. You're doing great," Benny said jauntily. He fit his stocky body comfortably into the niche she usually occupied and tilted his scruffy straw hat over his eyes.

The raft drifted peacefully. The others were out of sight around a bend, Rand and Jerry rowing more vigorously than Lark was. A hawk soared overhead, spiraling lazily on an updraft of warm air. A deer on shore lifted its head, interested but not fearful, to watch them slip silently by. The scream of jet motors didn't belong here, Lark thought. This was just the way it should be.

Lark was watching the deer more than the river, the oars lifted, when she suddenly became aware that the river beneath her feet had grown rough and bumpy. Alarmed, she looked ahead and gave a gasp as she saw a stretch of white-water rapids directly ahead.

"Benny!" she screamed as the first riffle caught the raft.

Benny leaped up as if he were on springs. His startled gaze took in the white-water ridges and hollows around them and the leaping, foaming stretch ahead. "I fell asleep!"

Benny struggled awkwardly over the supplies, clutching at the ropes. The raft danced and jerked as if some malevolent hand from below toyed with it. Lark fought with the oars, battling to keep the raft from swirling out of control until Benny could take over.

Then the raft hit a rock and bounced sideways, and in horror Lark saw Benny flung headfirst into the boiling water.

"Benny!" she screamed again, and then the treacherous rapids tossed the raft around as if it were an insignificant bauble, lifting it to the crest of a ridge of water and then flinging it into a jarring hollow. Lark clung to the oars, desperately dipping one to avoid a sharp snag of rock, rowing frantically to avoid another looming evil boulder. Stories of rafts caught and trapped helplessly by the current pushing against a rock swirled through her mind. She wasn't wearing a life jacket, and there was no time to stop and struggle into one.

And then finally she was on the other side, drifting gently on water incongruously smooth again, like a raging vixen suddenly changed to a demure lady. Lark lifted the oars and let her head slump weakly for a moment, but there was no time to rest or succumb to nerves. She had to find Benny! He hadn't been wearing a life jacket either.

She searched the frothing waters behind the raft. There he was! No, it was only an outcropping of rock. Then a cry and a frantically waving arm caught her attention, and somehow she managed to manhandle the raft in Benny's general direction as he was swept downstream. When she was a few feet away she thrust an oar toward him. He grabbed it and then with her help crawled over the smooth, rounded edge of the raft.

"Benny!" Lark gasped, terrified at the way he slumped over the piled supplies. "Are you all right?"

"Rand will kill me," Benny groaned. "What a dumb stunt to pull."

Lark glanced ahead. The other rafts were still out of sight. What Benny had done was foolish and could have been tragic in a raft filled with panicky passengers. But Lark had no doubt that Benny had learned his lesson thoroughly, and the only real casualty was his straw hat.

"Well, I have no intention of telling Rand anything," she said finally.

"Maybe you ought to take up guiding instead of working in the office," Benny said as he took over the oars. "You came through that rapids as if you'd been running the river all your life."

"No, thanks," Lark said shakily. "I think I'll stick to the safety of my typewriter."

She clambered back to her usual niche. She felt shaken and yet oddly pleased with herself. Benny's praise that she had handled the rapids as if she had been running the river all her life was a bit exaggerated, of course. It had been a very minor rapids, actually, compared to many they had been through. But she still felt good about it. She hadn't panicked. She hadn't even fallen apart after the crisis was over. She'd kept her head and looked out for Benny. Rand would have been proud of her.

Abruptly she dropped that thought as the boat drifted along, Benny rowing energetically through the slower-moving stretches of water because they had fallen so far behind the others. What Rand thought no longer mattered. But it did matter, she thought slowly, what she thought about herself.

Rand was gone, lost to her. There was no denying or escaping that. She would always regret the mistakes she had made that had cost her his love. But she was a better, stronger, more self-confident and self-reliant person for having known and loved him. Living without him wouldn't be easy. Some small part of her would always wish it could have been otherwise. But she would survive. The future was still there, however bleak it might appear at the moment.

Moreover, she realized slowly, there was one person she would always have to face in that future: herself. And as she thought about that, she also realized that she didn't like what she was doing, running out on the Hammonds in mid-season, shirking her commitment to them. Rand hadn't run out on his commitment, even though it had been difficult for him. He had even swallowed his stubbornness and compromised with his grandfather when he probably could have forced the ailing man to give in to his wishes. And neither would she run out on her responsibilities, she decided resolutely. She would swallow her loss and face life from there.

The decision lifted a nagging weight of guilt from her shoulders, and she was feeling almost happy by the time they caught up with the other rafts. They were already pulled into shore, the occupants impatiently waiting for the supply raft to arrive so camp could be set up. Benny's drenched condition drew some curious questions and teasing, but he managed to detour explaining what had really happened.

It was still early in the day, and hot, and Lark went swimming along with the others. The guides and some of the stronger swimmers went out in the deeper water, daringly letting the powerful current sweep them along, but Lark stayed in the shallow backwater, wading more than swimming. There was an interesting rock formation down the river a short distance, and after dressing in the concealing shrubbery, Lark headed toward the huge rock alone.

Before long she began to regret her desire to see the view from the rock. She had to climb well up the hillside to reach it, and the way was blocked by a jumbled debris of logs left by some rampaging flood of the past, piled up with rocks and boulders of varying size. Lizards, sunning themselves on the warm rocks, scurried out of her way, and once she heard the sound of some larger animal crashing through the underbrush above her.

Lark was perspiring freely by the time she paused to rest beneath a hip-high log angled across the rough slope. She was startled to hear footsteps crunch behind her. She looked around to see Rand only a short distance back of her. He must have gained on her rapidly, she thought, because he had just been getting out of the water when she started toward the rock. She tried to calm the distracting flip-flop of her heart, telling herself that their taking the same course was surely only accidental. Rand had changed to his usual Levi's, but his tanned chest was bare. Lark edged to one side to let him pass, but instead he stopped beside her.

"You've been avoiding me," he stated bluntly, his eyes roaming appraisingly over her bare legs. When Lark didn't comment, he changed the subject abruptly. "Are you enjoying the trip?"

"Oh, yes. It's marvelous!" Lark was relieved that he evidently intended to make impersonal conversation rather than some awkward scene. They were well above the level of the camp here. Below, the big yellow-and-black rafts looked like children's toys. The yells and laughter of happy people enjoying themselves drifted up the steep hillside. "Though I think Benny takes a certain delight in hitting the roughest part of the rapids just to get me all wet. I'm looking forward to Mule Creek Canyon tomorrow. Benny says it's like a long, twisting hallway cut through solid rock. Rather eerie, he says."

Rand nodded. "I think Blossom Bar beyond Mule Creek Canyon is the most exciting part of the trip. Tricky navigating through the boulders."

The icy tension between them thawed a fraction as they talked about the river, but when the subject was exhausted, and they were silent, Lark was once again uncomfortable.

"Don't let me keep you from wherever you were going," she murmured.

"I was following you," Rand said unexpectedly, and she eyed him warily. "There's something I wanted to say to you."

Lark noted that he didn't phrase it that he wanted to talk with her about something. Oh, no! He was as arrogant as ever; he had something to say to her and obviously expected her to stand there meekly and listen. Suddenly angry, she deliberately turned away and scrambled up on the big log. In one smooth jump Rand was beside her, his hand roughly grabbing her arm as they balanced precariously.

"I think everything has been said," she said coldly.

He ignored that, ignored her attempt to pull out of his grasp as well. "You're not along on this trip just because it's the Hammonds' policy to let lodge employees take a river trip sometime during the season." He paused, and there was an angry, accusing glitter in his eyes. "You're leaving, aren't you?"

"What makes you think that?" Lark evaded.

"Pam got hold of me and told me. She thought it was something I should know."

So he had known all along! "Pam had no right . . ." Lark choked over the words. What else had Pam told him? That she was moping around, pining away for love of him? She stared at him, shame and humiliation washing over her. He had made it brutally plain that whatever feelings he'd had for her had died, and yet Pam had told him . . .

Suddenly she jerked away from him and stumbled blindly toward the rock ledge on the far side of the log.

"Watch out!"

Lark barely heard the cry before she was flung roughly aside, one arm and knee hitting the log as she fell. Too stunned to be angry at the rough shove, she blinked and shook her head as she lifted herself up. In horror she saw the last half of a snake slithering off the rocky ledge, a half-dozen evil-looking button-shaped things on its tail. She gasped as she realized what it was. A rattlesnake! Rand had flung her aside just in time to avoid being bitten by the poisonous snake!

She stood up shakily. And then she saw at what cost Rand had saved her. He lay sprawled across the rocky ledge and log, facedown, arms outflung. He had evidently stepped toward the ledge, and then, as he desperately shoved her away from the snake, fallen and struck his head on the rock.

She dropped to her knees beside him. "Rand!" she cried. She searched frantically for a pulse at the tanned wrist, breathed easier when she found it, fast but steady. He moved groggily, and awkwardly she rolled him over on his back, lifting his foot where it was caught between log and ledge.

His pants leg was pushed up and his leg scraped where it had hit the rock, but it wasn't the raw skin which sent a stab of terror through Lark. It was the two small neat holes in the fleshy part of Rand's leg. The rattlesnake had bitten him! He had taken the strike meant for her.

She stared at the deadly marks, transfixed with shock. They were miles from a doctor and medical attention. But something had to be done, and done immediately. What? *What?* From somewhere in the depths of her memory she dredged up her father's instructions about snakebite when they lived in a rattlesnake-infested area of the Arizona desert. It came back to her now with the same horror she had felt when she first heard it. You had to take a knife and cut through the fang marks and then suck the blood and venom out before it could circulate through the victim and poison him.

Lark's mind reeled dizzily at the thought. A surge of nausea hit her and her throat constricted. She couldn't do it! Not cut flesh and suck blood and venom . . . Her stomach churned in revulsion.

But she had to do it. Rand shook his head groggily from the fall, not yet realizing what greater danger had befallen him. Lark steeled her nerves, fought down the nausea. What she did or didn't do right now could mean his life.

And for Rand she knew she could do anything.

But she had to have a knife! Without a knife she was helpless. Suddenly she remembered the pocketknife he always carried in his Levi's. Frantically she dug in his pockets. His body was still a limp weight on the ledge. Her fingers had just found the hard metal when he struggled to sit up.

"Don't move," she commanded crisply.

He blinked, eyeing the open pocketknife in her hands. "What are you doing?"

"The snake struck you on the leg when you pushed me out of the way. I've got to cut through the marks and suck the venom out."

She knelt by his exposed leg, the knife in her right hand as she gritted her teeth and steeled herself for what had to be done.

He put a restraining hand on her arm. "Wait . . ."

"It has to be done," she said grimly.

She put her other hand on the tanned leg, stretching the skin taut. Rand's hand moved up to her chin, forcing her eyes to meet his.

"You'd do this for me?" he said huskily.

"I love you," she said simply. Her humiliation and anger at the admission were gone. It was simply a fact now. She loved him and she would do this or anything else to save him.

"Lark, do you know why I'm on this trip?" he asked.

"You said Hank had to go after his trailer or something like that. It doesn't matter. We haven't much time. I have to—"

He grabbed her by both shoulders in spite of their awkward position. "It does matter! Hank went after his trailer at this particular time because I asked him to do it. Because I wanted to guide this trip."

"Why?" she asked, bewildered.

"Because Pam told me you were taking this trip before you went away."

Lark stared at him dumbly, lips parted in astonishment.

"There's a lot more I have to say to you, but first you'll have to run down to the raft and tell Benny what happened. Tell him to bring the snakebite kit. And ice." He looked deep into her eyes again. "And until we talk further, remember—I came on this trip because I couldn't stay away from you."

Lark looked blankly at the knife in her hand. Too much was coming at her all at once. Rand reached out and took the knife gently from her hand and leaned over to brush her cheek with his lips.

"I'll be all right," he soothed. "You just get Benny and the snakebite kit. There's time, if I don't move around."

Lark stared at him numbly a moment more before she abruptly came to her senses and clambered over the log. She raced headlong down the steep incline, scrambling over rocks and logs, ignoring branches slapping her face and scratching her bare arms. Somewhere, without even being aware she was doing it, she started screaming for Benny. He met her at the edge of the gravel bar, his stocky body still dripping from his swim.

Gasping, Lark explained what had happened. She was halfway afraid the happy-go-lucky Benny might panic, but he took charge immediately, racing for the first-aid kit in the boat and yelling to one of the other guides to bring ice from the food chest.

Lark started back up the hillside, but Benny passed her on the way, his stocky but muscular legs covering the rough ground with astonishing speed. By the time Lark reached the rocky ledge, Benny had already slit the skin of Rand's leg with the little razor-sharp instrument in the snakebite kit. He was applying suction to the cuts with a small rubber cup. Lark's stomach churned when she saw the blood, but she reached for Rand's hand and clutched it tightly, not speaking.

The other guide, Jerry, arrived with ice in a plastic bag. Benny instructed him to put it under and around the leg to retard circulation and slow absorption of the poison. Lark was unable to tell if Rand was in pain or not. His iron self-control served him well, and it was her hand, not his, that trembled uncontrollably.

She didn't know how long Benny worked with the suction cup. It seemed forever before she finally got up courage enough to ask, "Is he going to be all right now? There's no danger?"

"I think he'll be all right, but this is only a temporary measure," Benny said. He seemed to have grown up in the last few minutes. "We have to get him to a doctor as soon as possible. I'll take a raft and float on down to the lodge at Marial. It's only a few miles. I can call out from there for an emergency rescue helicopter to fly in."

Rand grinned. "You're doing fine, Benny. You'll make head guide yet."

Benny got a peculiar guilty look on his face and his glance darted to Lark. "There's something I'd better tell you—"

"Later," Lark said firmly. "Later."

Benny nodded and sternly instructed Rand to stay where he was and not try to move around, because movement encouraged blood circulation, and any remaining venom could be carried farther into the body.

The two young guides scrambled back down the slope. Jerry went to keep the guests calm. Lark watched as Benny started downstream alone in a raft, his arm lifted in a reassuring wave. She knew a moment of panic, thinking about what might happen if something went wrong, if he took a spill on the river. Then Rand gave her hand a little squeeze.

"He'll do fine," he said confidently. "The helicopter

will be here practically before you know it. All we have
to do now is wait."

Lark nodded and dipped her head to avoid letting him
see her tears of concern. She rhythmically worked the
little rubber suction cup as Benny had done. In spite of
Rand's calm reassurances, the wait and worry seemed
unbearable. All sorts of horrible "what-if" possibilities
kept darting through her mind. And there was nothing
she could do but work the suction cup and wait.

Rand watched her. "Not many girls would be willing
to try what you were planning to do to get the venom
out of my leg."

"I told you why," she said, a bit embarrassed at how
much she had revealed.

"But you're leaving."

Lark shook her head. "No. I was. I was running away
again."

"From me?"

"Yes!" She took a jerky breath. "But I changed my
mind. I thought I couldn't bear to be around things that
reminded me of . . . anyway, I wanted to run and hide,
but I . . . I have responsibilities and commitments here
that I won't run away from. I have to live with my own
conscience."

His fingers traced the line of her jaw, but she kept her
eyes averted, her attention trained on the small but all-
important rhythmic action of the suction cup.

"Perhaps I should be insulted that you've changed
your mind," he said. "It's rather flattering to think a
beautiful girl is so brokenhearted over me that she goes
racing off to God knows where. A little like a man dash-
ing off to join the Foreign Legion after a broken love affair."

Lark's blue eyes flashed at him, suspecting he was
making fun of her. "I don't think your ego needs that
kind of encouragement."

Unexpectedly he laughed. "You're right. To tell the
truth, I prefer a woman who is strong and self-reliant

enough to tell me to go to hell if that's what I deserve, rather than a woman who runs away in tears. And I have the feeling a real tongue-lashing is exactly what I deserve," he added huskily. "About that night on the lodge deck . . ."

He started to rise, and she pushed him back firmly. "Don't move."

"You can't admit that you love me and then expect me to lie there as if nothing had happened."

She glanced at him, a catch in her throat. "Does it . . . mean something to you?"

"Mean something?" he repeated. "I told you I came along on this trip because of you. I darn near had to bully Hank into going up to Portland to get his trailer."

"You didn't act as if you cared one way or the other at the beginning of the trip," she said slowly. "You seemed so indifferent."

"You've been indifferent too. I remember one time when I came in to tell you good-bye before I left on a river trip and you were typing away as if you couldn't care less that I was leaving."

She looked up at him in dismay. "You came to the office that day? But I thought . . ." She broke off, lower lip caught between her teeth, remembering, berating herself for that day. Perhaps what he had once said was right, she thought in a moment of self-loathing. Perhaps she was too much like devious, manipulating Gloria. She had desperately wanted to say good-bye to him that day, but she had hidden her feelings, feigned indifference. Oh, if only she could go back and change it all!

"It wasn't indifference," Lark said in a low voice, "even though it might have looked that way."

"And it wasn't indifference on my part at the start of this trip, either. I was afraid you might back off and not come at all if I did something to scare you off. I thought this might be my last chance to talk to you before you ran away."

"I'm not running!"

"I love you, Lark McIntyre," he suddenly said softly but distinctly, as if nothing else mattered. "I love you."

Lark's hands trembled on the little suction cup but she resolutely kept the rhythmic motion going. "The venom has gone to your head," she said shakily, her eyes on the slight swelling of his leg. "You don't know what you're saying."

"I know what I'm saying," he stated. "And if you don't look at me and believe me, I'm going to stand up and shake you until I shake some sense into you!"

Lark's eyes flew to meet his. "You mustn't move . . ."

He ignored that and reached for her, his powerful arms pulling her down on top of him. She could feel the full, muscular length of his solid body as his arms held her against him, and the warmth of his bare chest stole through her thin blouse. She looked down into his dark eyes and her heart pounded as she saw their smoldering depths.

"I love you," he said almost fiercely. "I didn't want to. I kept telling myself I didn't love you, that I didn't give a damn if you went away and I never saw you again. And then I realized I was scared as hell that you would really go. I'd go home to my house at night and it felt cold and empty and lonely. It never did before, but since that night you were there with me . . ." His arms tightened almost convulsively around her. "I love you."

"You would only have had to say a few words and I'd never have gone," Lark said tremulously.

"What words?"

"The words you just said," she admitted huskily.

Her blond hair fell on either side of his face like a curtain, closing their faces into a secret little world. He moved his hand up to caress the silky strands. She could feel his heart beating faster against her breasts, and sudden alarm made her pull back. Anything that increased his circulation was dangerous for him! She struggled as his arms held her tight, refusing to release her.

"You mustn't!" she gasped. "It's not good for you. If the venom gets in your bloodstream . . ."

"I'll die right here on the spot, and it will all be your fault."

"No!" She almost panicked, and then she looked down and saw the teasing, dancing lights in his dark eyes. Then she remembered the suction cup and what she was supposed to be doing. "I have to—"

"I won't let go of you and you can't do anything until you tell me one thing."

"Wh-what?"

"That you'll marry me."

He lifted his head to claim her lips, and Lark felt a giddy dizziness sweep through her. Her healthy young body responded and her lips moved against his with growing passion. She felt her body mold itself to his lean, hard contours. Then she realized in horror what she was doing as she felt the erratic thud of his heart. She pulled back, her arms straining against him. A heat that had nothing to do with the sunshine beating down shimmered around them.

"No, you mustn't . . ."

His arms only tightened. "You didn't answer my question."

"I'll marry you!"

He released her then, a satisfied smile on his lips. Shakily she went back to working with the suction cup as his hand caressed her slim waist possessively.

"I'm going with you when the helicopter comes," she suddenly said determinedly.

"I'm not sure there'll be room."

"They'll have to make room," she said. "I won't let them leave me behind."

He started to pull her into his arms again, but she shook her head warningly. "Later," she said huskily, promise in both her eyes and voice. Then she smiled and leaned over to brush her lips lightly across his temple, her eyes bright with tears of worry and love.

"You're going to miss the best part of the river trip if you fly out in the helicopter with me," he warned. "Mule Creek Canyon and Blossom Bar."

"I don't care," she said stubbornly. "I'm going with you."

He brushed her hair with his hand. "You won't miss anything, I promise you," he said huskily. "We'll be back, just the two of us. I'll show you the river as I've never shown it to anyone else." And with a wicked gleam of promise in his eyes, he added, "If we have time in between all the other things I intend to show you, my love."

RAPTURE ROMANCE

Provocative and sensual,
passionate and tender—
the magic and mystery of love
in all its many guises

(0451)

#1☐ LOVE SO FEARFUL by Nina Coombs. *Never have an affair with your boss!* That was the first rule of business Megan Ryan had learned. Yet right from the start, rodeo star Bart Dutton made it clear he wanted her—and not because his ranch desperately needed a veterinarian. She swore she wouldn't give in to him, but there was no denying the way his very presence weakened all her good intentions. (120035—$1.95)*

#2☐ RIVER OF LOVE by Lisa McConnell. To Lark McIntyre, tired of charming con men and adoring lovers, forceful, self-confident, coldly indifferent Rand Whitcomb was a challenge she couldn't resist. She didn't realize what a dangerous game she was playing until seducer became seduced and she was caught in her own passionate trap. (120043—$1.95)*

#3☐ LOVER'S LAIR by Jeanette Ernest. For golden-haired Adrian Anders to be held in Adam's arms was paradise. But then came rumors of his past. Was Adam keeping some scandalous secret from her? Was he using her for his own ruthless purposes? Adrian had to know the truth, even though it was almost too late to deny the passionate feelings rising within her.

(120051—$1.95)*

#4☐ WELCOME INTRUDER by Charlotte Wisely. Painter Louis Castillo meant more to Jean than even her art career, but she knew he used and set aside beautiful women like finished works of art. How could she believe that he saw her as anything more than the most recent in a long series of challenges?

(120078—$1.95)*

*Prices slightly higher in Canada

RAPTURE ROMANCE

Coming next month

CHESAPEAKE AUTUMN
by Stephanie Richards

Garth Logan had swept into Deirdre's life in one night of unforgettable passion—leaving her with an infant child and a marriage that was truly in name only. Now he was back . . . was it to recapture the timeless moment of love they had shared—or to claim the son she adored?

PASSION'S DOMAIN
by Nina Coombs

Auburn-haired Mickey Callahan had never met a man as infuriating as architect Greg Bennett. She had criticized his designs, refused to do business with him, told him she didn't need him, and still she could not deny that his least caress stirred her to the depths of her being. Mickey didn't surrender to anyone—but Greg wasn't asking permission to take what he wanted . . .

RAPTURE ROMANCE—*Reader's Opinion Questionnaire*

Thank you for filling out our questionnaire. Your response to the following questions will help us to bring you more and better books, by telling us what you are like, what you look for in a romance, and how we can best keep you informed about our books. Your opinions are important to us, and we appreciate your help.

1. What made you choose this particular book? (This book is #_____)
    Art on the front cover_____
    Plot descriptions on the back cover_____
    Friend's recommendation_____
    Other (please specify)_____

2. Would you rate this book:
    Excellent_____
    Very good_____
    Good_____
    Fair_____

3. Were the love scenes (circle answers):
    A. Too explicit   Not explicit enough   Just right
    B. Too frequent   Not frequent enough   Just right

4. How many Rapture Romances have you read?_____

5. Number, from most favorite to least favorite, romance lines you enjoy:
    Adventures in Love_____
    Ballantine Love and Life_____
    Bantam Circle of Love_____
    Dell Candlelight _____
    Dell Candlelight Ecstasy_____
    Jove Second Chance at Love_____
    Harlequin_____
    Harlequin Presents_____
    Harlequin Super Romance_____
    Rapture Romance_____
    Silhouette_____
    Silhouette Desire_____
    Silhouette Special Edition_____

6. Please check the *types* of romances you enjoy:
    Historical romance_____
    Regency romance_____
    Romantic suspense_____
    Short, light contemporary romance_____
    Short, sensual contemporary romance_____
    Longer contemporary romance_____

7. What is the age of the oldest _____ youngest _____ heroine you would like to read about? The oldest _____ youngest _____ hero?

8. What elements do you dislike in a romance?
   Mystery/suspense_____
   Supernatural_____
   Other (please specify) _____
9. We would like to know:
   - How much television you watch
       Over 4 hours a day_____
       2–4 hours a day_____
       0–2 hours a day_____
   - What your favorite programs are
       _____
       _____
   - When you usually watch television
       8 a.m. to 5 p.m._____
       5 p.m. to 11 p.m._____
       11 p.m. to 2 a.m._____
10. How many magazines do you read regularly?
    More than 6_____
    3–6_____
    0–3_____
    Which of these are your favorites?
    _____
    _____

To get a picture of our readers, and to know where to reach
them, the following personal information will be most helpful, if
you don't mind giving it, and will be kept only for our records.

Name _____   Please check your age
Address_____   group:
City _____   17 and under_____
State_____ Zip code_____   18–34_____
                                     35–49_____
                                     50–64_____
                                     64 and older_____

Education: Are you now working
   Now in high school_____   outside the home?
   Now in college_____   Yes_____ No_____
   Graduated from high school_____   Full time_____
   Completed some college_____   Part time_____
   Graduated from college_____   Job title_____

Thank you for your time and effort. Please send the com-
pleted questionnaire and answer sheet to: Robin Grunder,
RAPTURE ROMANCE, New American Library, 1633 Broadway,
New York, NY 10019